Ashbel Woodward, Franklin C. Jones

Celebration of the one Hundred and Fiftieth Anniversary

Of the primitive organization of the Congregational church and society, in Franklin,

Connecticut, October 14th, 1868

Ashbel Woodward, Franklin C. Jones

Celebration of the one Hundred and Fiftieth Anniversary
Of the primitive organization of the Congregational church and society, in Franklin, Connecticut, October 14th, 1868

ISBN/EAN: 9783337234553

Printed in Europe, USA, Canada, Australia, Japan

Cover: Foto ©Andreas Hilbeck / pixelio.de

More available books at **www.hansebooks.com**

MAP
(of)
NORWICH
West Farms
1663-1725.

THE

CELEBRATION

OF THE

ONE HUNDRED AND FIFTIETH

ANNIVERSARY

OF THE

PRIMITIVE ORGANIZATION

OF THE

Congregational Church and Society,

IN

FRANKLIN, CONNECTICUT,

OCTOBER 14th, 1868.

TUTTLE, MOREHOUSE & TAYLOR, PRINTERS,
NEW HAVEN.
1869.

NOTE.—The accompanying map gives the location of the first settlers of Franklin. It covers a period extending from 1663, when the lands of West Farms were partly apportioned among the Original Proprietors of Norwich, to 1725, by which time the population had become tolerably numerous. In the Historical Address and in its appended notes, the reader will find the time and order of arrival of these settlers. The present inhabitants will also perceive by a glance at the map who were the first owners of the farms which they now occupy, and, if they are curious to follow up the clue thus furnished, they can, by consultation of the records, trace the succession of owners down to themselves. The various names of places then in vogue are also given. Some of these are still retained, while others have been long in disuse.

The preparation of this map has involved a vast amount of labor. It is the result of investigations extending over a series of years, and to which the writer was led in connection with other historical studies. In its preparation the early deeds of the town of Norwich have been minutely explored, as well as a great number of private papers and deeds in the possession of different families. The series of papers on file in the State Library have also afforded valuable assistance. Not a little information has also been obtained from the examination of the ordinary records of the same date, which, in their records of votes respecting particular sections of the town, of allotments to different individuals, of the location of roads, of the running of district lines, &c., &c., have incidentally furnished decisive evidence. By the collation of these different authorities facts have been elicited which could not have been obtained from any single source. No location has been given which is not supported either by the direct evidence of the deeds or by strong collateral evidence.

The map may claim, therefore, to present a truthful representation of the town during the first half century of its history, and the writer ventures to hope that this study of a former generation will afford to the present one a pleasure equal to that which it has given to himself.　　　　　A. W.

CONTENTS.

———•••———

———•◆•———

ADDITIONS AND CORRECTIONS.

On page 23, the 16th line from the top, for 1610 read 1710.
On page 37, the 5th line from the top, for 1608 read 1708.
On page 43, the 7th line from the top, for Edward read Ezra.
On page 51, the 16th line from the top, for Get-once read Yet-once.
On page 56, the 19th line from the top, for she read he.
On page 78, the last line, add the character £ so as to read £3.

PRELIMINARY MEETINGS.

At a meeting of the Congregational church of Franklin, Conn., August 30th, 1867, it was voted to celebrate the approaching one hundred and fiftieth anniversary of its organization with appropriate exercises, and the following committee were appointed to make the necessary arrangements:—Ashbel Woodward, M. D., Chairman ; Joseph I. Hyde, Clerk ; P. O. Smith, H. W. Kingsley and Dan Hastings. The Ecclesiastical Society voted unanimously, September 30th, 1867, to commemorate its own organization in conjunction with the celebration of the one hundred and fiftieth anniversary of the church.

At a subsequent meeting of the committee of arrangements, Rev. Franklin C. Jones was invited to deliver the Historical Sermon, and Ashbel Woodward, M. D., the Historical Address. It was also voted to hold the anniversary celebration on Wednesday, October 7th, 1868.*

September 13th, 1868, the committee of arrangements appointed the following special committees :

On Collation.—Herman H. Willes, Amos F. Royce, Wm. M. Converse, Charles A. Kingsley, James C. Woodward, Ezra L. Smith and E. Eugene Ayer.

---

* It subsequently became known that the American Board of Commissioners for Foreign Missions were to hold their annual meeting at Norwich city during the first week of October, 1868, and it was, therefore, deemed advisable to defer the anniversary exercises till the second Wednesday of October. Fortunately the organization of the church took place on the second Wednesday of October, 1718, and we were thereby enabled in a certain sense to celebrate upon the anniversary of the date of its organization, although there was an actual discrepancy of one week ; the celebration occurring October 14, while the organization took place October 8th.

On Finance.—William B. Hyde, John O. Smith, Bela T. Hastings, Amos F. Royce and Lavius A. Robinson.

On Reception.—Henry W. Kingsley, Oliver L. Johnson, Lovell K. Smith, Samuel G. Hartshorn, Owen S. Smith, Ezra L. Smith, Dan Hastings and Charles A. Kingsley.

On Music.—Hezekiah Huntington, Prentice O. Smith and Rev. F. C. Jones.

Anniversary Exercises.

———•◆•———

The morning of October 14th, 1868, opened with threatening clouds and damp, cutting winds. But, notwithstanding the inauspicious weather, the church was crowded at an early hour with the returning sons and daughters of Franklin, some of whom had journeyed from beyond the Mississippi to join in the festivities of the day, while others had come back gray-haired men to once more grasp hands with the playmates with whom they had parted half a century before.

At half-past ten o'clock, the Hon. Ephraim H. Hyde, of Stafford, Lieutenant Governor of Connecticut, was introduced as president of the day, by the pastor, and the exercises of the occasion were opened with an invocation by Rev. E. W. Gilman.

The following hymn, written by Miss F. M. Caulkins, of New London, was then sung by the Choir.

OPENING HYMN

*For the Celebration of the 150th Anniversary of the first Organization
of Religious Worship in Franklin, Conn.*

BY MISS F. M. CAULKINS.

Church of our fathers, hail!
Long on this sacred height,
Thy shining courts o'er hill and dale
Have shed celestial light.

A few worn pilgrims here
Their altar reared to God:
Here first the *Burning-bush* they saw,
Here bloomed the *Almond rod*.

The watchmen of the land,
　　Like stars before us rise :—
For seventy years one faithful hand
　　Was pointed to the skies.

And still thy garments shine,
　　With plenteous grace bedewed :
Rich are the clusters of thy vine,
　　Thy sons a multitude.

For blessings so supreme,
　　Our grateful songs we raise ;
Lift high, sound deep the joyful theme,
　　Awake, O voice of Praise !

Now, Lord, in triumph come !
　　Here shed thy spirit free,
That each may bear a blessing home
　　From this, our jubilee.

After the singing of the opening hymn, the chairman of the committee of arrangements, Ashbel Woodward. M. D., delivered the following

ADDRESS OF WELCOME.

— ⋅♦⋅ —

SONS AND DAUGHTERS OF FRANKLIN:—

IN behalf of the committee of arrangements for cele-
brating this anniversary occasion, I greet you with a
cordial welcome. It affords me no ordinary gratification
to welcome you to a full participation in all the pleasant
memories and amenities which this hallowed re-union is
suited to call forth. I welcome you to the hospitalities
of our homes, which were once the homes of your fathers
and your fathers' fathers. And to all who have upon this
auspicious morning favored us by your presence, I would
extend the warmest welcome of our hearts.

It is profitable to turn aside occasionally from the stir-
ring scenes of the hour to contemplate the virtues of those
who have lived before us. No people can become permanently great and prosperous unless they revere the
memory of a virtuous ancestry. This feeling underlies
the sentiment of patriotism and inspires the self-devotion
of the hero. If the Roman of the empire was not ashamed
to acknowledge his descent from the robber band who
founded the eternal city ; if the Briton proudly traces his
lineage to the Danish and Saxon pirates of the mediaeval
period, surely we may well rejoice that our blood is de-
rived from a religious, heroic, God-fearing ancestry.
Amid perils and privations they sowed the precious seed,
upborne by a lofty faith even in the darkest hours of trial
and adversity. Reflecting upon the piety, and courage,

and resolution of our fathers who laid the foundations here, we shall not only appreciate more fully the greatness of their work, but be the better fitted to carry it onward toward final fulfillment.

Our town, secluded and sparsely settled by an agricultural people, has borne an unconspicuous part in history. Yet she has given to the country not a few who have risen to high positions of honor and usefulness. Trained in the virtues of the puritans, her sons and their descendants have ennobled this, their birth-place.

But not to detain you with further words, allow me to extend to you, one and all, the earnest and sincere welcome of our hearts.

The address of welcome was succeeded by reading of the scriptures, Isaiah xxxv, and prayer by Rev. H. P. Arms, D. D.

After further singing by the choir, came the Historical Address.

HISTORICAL ADDRESS,

ASHBEL WOODWARD, M. D.

Introductory Note.

The author of the following address is unwilling to permit this memorial volume to go to press without acknowledging that its tardy appearance is due almost entirely to himself. Actively devoted to a profession which precludes all system in the improvement of moments devoted to non-professional research, he has only been enabled to seize upon detached fragments of time to accomplish the little that was originally contemplated.

In preparing the accompanying notes, almost constant recourse has been had to the *local records*, which fortunately are full and in a good state of preservation. All the early papers now on file in the public offices at the State Capitol, relating to our history in colonial times, have been examined and much valuable information has been obtained therefrom.

The late Miss F. M. Caulkins, in collecting materials for her invaluable *History of Norwich*, availed herself of all known sources of information, and left comparatively little for other gleaners. Frequent reference has been had to her writings, which have afforded very valuable aid in the preparation of these sketches.

The writer also feels greatly indebted to the late chancellor Walworth, not only for information which he kindly furnished as a correspondent, but for many important statistical facts embodied in his *Genealogy of the Hyde Family*, a work involving vast labor, and including in its scope many of the families resident in this place.

He also feels under great obligations to Rev. Dr. Sprague, of Albany, for information communicated by letter, and for the aid afforded by his printed volumes.

He would also acknowledge information furnished by Rev. Jesse Fillmore, of Providence, Rev. F. B. Huntington, of Stamford, Prof. Gilman and F. B. Dexter, of Yale College, and others.

He would also add that he feels under great obligations to Hon. J. H. Trumbull, President of the Conn. Historical Society, for assistance upon the obscure subject of Indian names.

The mechanical execution of the accompanying map was entrusted to Mr. Andrew B. Smith, Post Master at Franklin.

Franklin, April 14th, 1869.

HISTORICAL ADDRESS.

THE Society whose anniversary we celebrate to-day, embraces territory purchased of the Indians in the month of June, 1659. Originally this region lay within the domain of the Narragansett, but he, at some unknown period, was driven back by the irruption of a fierce tribe from the north, who swept down with an impetuosity which even his might could not withstand. These new comers, settling upon the banks of the stream afterwards called by their name, the Pequot or Thames, issued forth from thence conquering and to conquer, a living terror far and near, until overwhelmed in the memorable destruction of 1637. The Mohegans, an uneasy clan of the Pequots and a traitorous aid in their overthrow, rose Phœnix-like from the ruins of their race, and had become in 1659 a powerful tribe dwelling about the headwaters of the Thames and extending thence into the interior. Their territory was the fairest in New England. Nature here lavished in stream and vale the means of easy subsistence, while in scenes of rugged grandeur ceaselessly blending with others of quiet repose, she spoke in such tones of captivating eloquence to her first children as she does to-day to those who have ears to listen. But nowhere in this broad domain was her hand more generous or her smile more winsome than over the region which greets the eye from the spot whereon we stand. Here pure streams, flowing with increased volume beneath the shade of the primeval forest, sparkled through valleys from whose genial soil the three sister spirits, guardians of the red man's board, the spirit of Corn, of the Bean and of the Vine, drew the kindliest support. Over the hills above, ranged the deer, bear, wolf and fox, while the encircling streams furnished still choicer food in their abundant supplies of salmon, shad and trout. Here, then, was joy to the full for the red man, and the abundant remains of his art join with tradition in pronouncing this his favorite abode. In these valleys, long before they felt the white man's tread, the summer wind rustled through the complaining corn, the woods re-echoed to the huntsman's joyous shout, or anon the war-whoop rung out from hill to hill, and the streams ran red with blood. Again, where, perhaps, this very church rears heavenward its spire, weird companies have circled round the council fire in celebration of their mystic rites, or in the golden harvest time, led by the gratitude which yearly draws us nither, have gathered from far and near to return thanks to the Great Spirit for bounteous seasons, and to bespeak his continued kindness. But this aboriginal form of society, with its bright alike with its dark side, be it spoken, vanished so quickly away that only the faintest glimpses of it are preserved for us, and we hasten on into more certain periods.

Doubtless the people of Saybrook were familiar with the charms and advantages of this region long before a colony was actually led hither. Major John Mason, the leading spirit in that settlement, had had abundant opportunity in his frequent expeditions through the wilderness and his long intimacy with Uncas, to learn the nature of the sachem's possessions; and it was doubtless the enthusiastic admiration of this tireless man that prevailed upon his fellow colonists to abandon their homes, just beginning to requite the toil of years, and plunge again into the heart of the wilderness.

In May, 1659, the General Assembly authorized the planting of a colony in the Mohegan country ; and the following month Uncas and his brother Wawequa, for the consideration of seventy pounds, ceded a portion of their domain nine miles square, and including within its limits the present towns of Norwich, Franklin, Bozrah, Lisbon and Sprague, with small portions of adjoining towns.

Preliminary arrangements are at once effected, and the next spring the thirty-five proprietors, under the guidance of Major Mason and Rev. James Fitch, remove from Saybrook hither, and establish themselves at what is now known as Norwich Town. The first year or two are busily employed in erecting dwellings and subduing the wilderness about them. These done, other matters press upon the attention. Young men are growing up in their midst, full of the energy begotten by struggles with nature in a new land, who will quickly be ready to plunge still deeper into the shades of the forest, there to hew out their own fortunes. New comers, also, from abroad must soon be crowded onward beyond the existing bounds, while the needs of the present population suggest the clearing up of outlying lands for pasturage and cultivation. The meadows and uplands of West Farms, as this portion of Norwich was long known, are most accessible and inviting. Accordingly, in *Sixteen Hundred and Sixty-Three*, the desirable portions are parcelled out among the occupants of the Town Plot, to be improved by them, or, if they see fit, passed over into other hands. Nor is it long before the smoke curls up here and there from the center of a little clearing, in indication of actual occupation. Soon John Ayer, the famous hunter, Indian fighter and guide, pushes up the Beaver brook and pitches

his tent in the gap of the hills, a wild and solitary place
exactly to his taste and perpetuating by its name the
memory of his many daring exploits in its vicinity. Job
Hunnewell, William Moore and others, follow in his
footsteps, and settle up and down the different streams.
These first comers, unused to the restraints of civilization,
when, in a few years, neighbors begin to crowd upon them,
sigh again for the freedom of the forest, and most of them
pass on into the unbroken wilderness. Yet these same
men were the actual pioneers in the settlement of West
Farms, and carry back the history of this portion of the
nine miles square almost to the days of the original settlement at the Town Plot. Nearly coeval with the arrival
of these men here, Samuel Hyde, John Birchard,
John Johnson and John Tracy move out from the
Town Plot and settle upon the lands that fell to them in
the division of 1663.

Two hundred years ago! Who of us can realize the
change, or depict the life of those adventurous men, here
in the very heart of the wilderness, shut in on every side
by the gloom of the primeval forest, and environed by
countless perils? From the surrounding shades savage
beasts are ready to pounce upon their herds and
trample down their crops, or, at some unguarded moment,
the war-whoop may ring out the death knell of unpro-
tected wives and children. Life is a constant struggle
with hardship and danger. Scarcely are the toilsome
beginnings over and a slight degree of comfort attained,
when King Phillip's war bursts forth, to rage with uninterrupted fury for many months, The compacted settle-
ments are stricken with deadly fear. Young and old rush
to arms. Heavy guards are maintained night and day.
Yet with the utmost vigilance a forlorn dread settles upon
every heart; dread lest their stoutest defences avail not

against the wiles of the Narragansett chief. What, then, must be the feelings, the sickening despair of the lonely family upon the frontier, cut off from the assistance of neighbors and friends, and to whom the appearance of the foe is the precursor of inevitable death; death, too, under all the tortures that devilish cunning can devise? We, whose fortunes have fallen upon peaceful times, but faintly realize the horrors of those early days. No woman in the absence of her husband at his daily toil, could feel sure that in his stead a mangled corpse would not come back to her at night. No father in parting from his wife and children could shake off the dread that his returning footsteps might bring him to smouldering ruins and the charred remains of dear ones. Life was a burthen, to be flung off with joy but for the interests of others bound up in it. Amid such scenes did the fathers lay the foundations of our goodly town, and many of our richest blessings are due to the heroic spirit that could endure and grow strong by battling with adversity.

With the downfall of King Phillip, in 1676, sank the last great Indian power in New England. Peace is now assured, and under her fostering influences the West Farms receive fresh life. The next year Joshua Abel removes from Dedham hither, and establishes himself at the foot of the hill, directly below our present church. Benjamin and John Armstrong, Nathaniel Rudd and others follow rapidly, and the place soon begins to wear the air of civilization. Before 1690, crops of grain wave over many a field but lately torn from the embrace of the forest, wood-paths have expanded into highways—one leading to Portipaug, one up the central valley and over Middle hill, and another along the long and elevated crest, then known as Little Lebanon—and the victories of civilization over barbarism appear on every hand. A glance at

the surrounding country will, perhaps, place the antiquity
of the West Farms in clearer light. While they already
boast a thriving and populous community, rapidly extending their conquests over nature, other ancient towns that
hold early and honorable place in the annals of the State,
have not yet come into existence. Windham is still Nau-
besetuck, or, at most, contains but a single log cabin, and
Lebanon is an unbroken wilderness. Even over the nine
miles square, save about the Town Plot, there are elsewhere only a few straggling settlers. In this vicinity
Franklin claims an actual history, antedated only by the
settlement at the Town Plot.

Each returning year brings its additions to the population. Among others, one after another, the names of
Hyde, Birchard, Edgerton, Smith, Waterman, Huntington, Tracy, Royce, Gager and Mason are added
to the list, all sons or connected with the first proprietors, and so many links to bind more closely together
the communities of the Town Plot and the West Farms,
though, in fact, they are already as one people, gathering
in the same church, forming a single civil body, and
marching forth shoulder to shoulder wherever the duties
of those warlike days might call. Indeed, until the final
separation in 1786, though to a less degree after the formation of this Society, the history of Franklin is to be
found in the history of Norwich. Her inhabitants constitute no small portion of the body politic, have a voice in
all civil matters, bear off their portion of the offices and
their full share of the heavy burthens consequent upon
early citizenship. If their history be merged in the history of the older and larger town, we must not forget
that they have a history, nay, occupy an important place
in the annals of the period.

Yet, in face of these blending influences, it will not

seem strange that the people of the West Farms should
soon tire of a straggling existence upon the outskirts of a
distant society, and long for greater independence. After
several years of fruitless effort, their wishes are at length
gratified by permission, in 1716, to organize a separate
Ecclesiastical Society. But, before passing to the new
organization, shall we hastily glance at this locality a century and a half ago? It is jocularly called the " Place of
the Seven Hills," and though most of their different names
have long been in disuse, the hills still tower up in silent
witness of the peculiar fitness of the term. On the east
stands Portipaug hill, flanked on one side by Pleasure hill
and on the other by Hearthstone hill, so called from its
excellent hearthstones; from the center rises Center or
Middle (now Great) hill, noted for its Dragon's Hole*
and the picturesqueness of the surrounding scenery ; west

* We subjoin the following description of this natural curiosity from a manuscript account by Rev. Dr. Nott. " August 5, 1800, I went, in company with
Rev. John Ellis and four students, to view the Dragon's Hole. The ascent of
the mountain from the east is laborious for about a quarter of a mile. The mouth
of the cavern is between two ledges of rocks, that on the right being about
35 feet in height and the left one about 20. The space between them is about
30 feet, and covered with rocks of various shapes and sizes thrown together
in such a manner as to bring to mind those lines more celebrated for wit than
piety—

       ' Nature, having spent all her store,
       ' Heaped up rocks—she could do no more.'

The descent from the general surface of those promiscuous rocks to the mouth
of the cavern is about 10 feet. The first room, which is something in the form
of a parallelogram, is 12 feet in length, 9 in breadth, and 6 in height. The
passage from the first to the second room is 9 feet long, 3 1-2 high, and 2 wide.
The second room is not so large. Its length is 9 1-2 feet, width 4, and height
6 feet. From the second room there is an opening to two others, one on the
right, the other on the left. The one on the right is 5 feet high, 7 1-2 long,
and 3 1-2 wide. The room on the left is 5 feet high, 9 long, and 4 wide.
From this there is a narrow passage on the left into which my son entered,
12 feet in length and 2 in width. From one extremity of the cavern to the
other is about 40 feet."

of Middle is what is now known as Meeting House hill,
looming up above its neighbors, in seeming forgetfulness
of the doubtful honor of the sobriquet of Misery hill,
sometimes applied to its southern terminus; beyond this
lies Little Lebanon, and still farther west, Blue hill com-
pletes the mystic seven.

To one gazing off from this Meeting House hill, or
journeying hence in different directions, the prospect is
essentially that which greets the eye to-day. True, the
roads are not so easy, or the lands so smooth, or the
dwellings so comfortable and commodious as now.
Blackened stumps still protrude from many a clearing.
The log cabin has not yet begun its westward march, and
occasionally a wigwam peeps out from some sunny nook,
or Ashbow and his clan are seen pursuing their game
across the fields. No church spire bids the dwellers in
these valleys lift their thoughts toward heaven. No
grave-yard whitens yonder plain. Nor are there school
houses yet at every turn, New England's mighty enginery,
destined in the course of time to revolutionize the world.
Perhaps one of us transported back to this early day
would be struck most by the Great Pine Swamp, an
immense extent of pines skirting the eastern base of
Meeting House hill, and spreading out through the whole
length and breadth of the valley. Yet, after all, the
changes which these hundred and fifty years have wrought,
are not so great that we should fail to recognize our
honored town or cease to feel at home within her borders.
The cultivated lands are, mainly, the same as now; the
farm houses occupy the same positions; nay, if we knock
for entrance, a cordial welcome awaits us from the grand-
fathers and great-grandfathers of those who preside over
the self same hearths to-day. Starting near the Society
line and going north, the traveler first passes the residence

Samuel Nott

of Capt. Joseph Tracy, a grandson of Lieut. Thomas
Tracy, and ancestor of the late Dr. Philemon Tracy.
If he chances to take the Portipaug road he will soon
pass the residence of Serj. Nathaniel Rudd; then that of
Samuel Hartshorne, situated upon the spot occupied
by successive generations of the family to the present
day; next that of Lieut. Thomas Hazen, under the
family name till recently; and at the head of the lane,
upon the right, the homestead of Dr. David Hartshorne,
father of Samuel Hartshorne below, the first physician
of the society, and a most exemplary man; he then passes
successively, the houses of Benjamin and John Armstrong; and if he still keeps to the right he will pass the
place of Capt. John Fillmore, ancestor of President
Fillmore, and noted for his encounter with the pirates;
and, near by, the residence of Samuel Griswold; and
finally cross the Shetucket at Elderkin's (now Lord's)
bridge, near which lives John Elderkin, and are located
the saw and gristmill for that section; or, taking the *left*
hand road, winding around through Portipaug, he passes,
among others, the places of Increase Mosely, Doctor
John Sabin, and Joseph Ayer and his son Joseph; and
climbing upon Pleasure hill, finds there the farms of
Jacob Hyde and David Ladd. Returning to the starting point and following the Windham road, our traveler
passes at Rudd hill what soon became the residence of
Nathaniel Rudd, Jr.; soon observes at a short distance
upon the right, that of the 1st Thomas Hyde, and a little
farther off that of John Pember, afterwards society
sexton, as were his son and grandson after him; and still
farther on in that direction, upon Birchard's plain, the
residence of James Birchard; reaches at the foot of
Middle hill the house of Joshua Abell, and, climbing
the hill by the old and tortuous way, the more direct

route being yet unopened, passes on the ascent John Badger, at the top, the Kingsbury Mansion, and so successively, Serj. Winslow Tracy, William Hogskin, John Gager, Jonathan Hartshorne, a brother of David, Joseph Downer and Joseph Reynolds. Returning southward and journeying up Lebanon road, our traveler first passes the home of Serj. Obadiah Smith, and still farther along, at the foot of Little Lebanon hill, that of Jabez Hyde, first clerk of the society; ascending the hill, that of Samuel Crocker, from whom that portion of the hill now takes its name; at the top of the hill, the Huntington mansion, then occupied by Christopher Huntington; farther on, John Tracy; next, Joseph Edgerton; and farther on, at the other end of the hill, the first Jeremiah Mason. Returning into West Farms by the Blue hill road, he passes on Blue hill the farms of Samuel Pettis, Serj. Israel Lathrop and Ebenezer Johnson; then, descending through the Hollow, and passing the mill of Thomas Sluman, and on the ascent, the farm of the mysterious Micah Rood, he finds on the brow of Meeting House hill, the Capt. John Lothrup place, and still farther on, in front of our present parsonage, the then Arnold place, afterwards occupied by Rev. Henry Willes, and upon the opposite corner, the dwelling of Benjamin Peck. Nor are these all. During his tour the dwellings of many others have caught his eye, some of them not unknown to us, though of less interest to the present generation, the rest long since forgotten. More than once, perhaps, in his walk, he has been startled by the warning of the rattlesnake; or, if his visit fall in spring time, urged to join in the annual expeditions against these terrible pests of the settlement.* Lingering awhile,

---

* Rattlesnakes were for many years *the* pest of the settlement. It is said that they nearly frightened away the first settler at Portipaug by their frequent

he will find ample chance for nobler sport in the frequent
forays against the bears and wolves, still numerous enough
to endanger the safety of the herds. Would that in his
stead we might tarry for a time, and, gathering round
some cheerful hearth, observe the homely, though genial
customs of the day, learn of the topics that interest our
sturdy sires, and be quickened in fidelity to conviction,
by the story of their own and their fathers' heroic
struggles to maintain the truth.

It will be seen from this survey, that the West Farms
are at length fully prepared for a more independent existence. They now number nearly fifty families,* and the
burthens of connection with a society whose center is so
distant are far greater than would be those of maintaining
a separate organization, while the benefits are correspond-
ingly less. As early as 1610 the discontent with the
existing arrangement creates a strong desire for a new
township, and finds actual expression in a petition to the
town for leave to organize a separate society. For some
reason no definite action is taken upon this petition.
But six years later the project is crowned with success.

On the nineteenth of September, 1716, the inhabitants
of the town of Norwich agree in general town meeting,
"that the West Farmers be allowed to be a society by
themselves."† The next step is to secure incorporation
by the General Assembly, and to this end the following
petition is preferred to that body :—

---

visits to his cabin. For a long time a large bounty was offered for their
destruction, and several of the early days of May were annually devoted to
hunting them.

* Several families are known to have been here at this time who are unrep-
resented on the petition to the General Assembly.

† Upon ye petition of ye West Farmers in Nowich, pleading to be a society
by themselves, the inhabitants now met in general Town meeting, September
19th, 1716. And having considered sd Petition, do agree yt ye sd West

To the Honour[ble] the Govern[r], Council & Representatives in General Court, assembled at New Haven, October 11th, 1716.

May it please y[r] Hon[rs].

We, the inhabitants of the town of Norwich, comonly called the West Farmers of Norwich, Having obtained the consent of sd town, to be a distinct society, after having the allowance of this Hon[ble] Court; as appears by their vote dated Septemb[r] 19th, 1716, Do now pray y[r] Hon[rs] to grant and constitute us a distinct society, according to the line agreed upon in the above referred to vote, with those privileges and imunities, which to y[r] wisdom shall seem needful to the promoting the end of our being a separate society. And herein we have great hopes of the favor of this Hon[ble] Assembly, forasmuch as the flourishing of religion is our only motive, upon the publick institutions of which it is scarce possible for us to attend in Norwich, being several of us seven or eight & but two or three within four miles of the place of publick worship.

And to this application to y[r] Hon[rs] we are also encouraged by the smiles of Providence in increasing our inhabitants to the number of above forty families & trust that by the continuance of the same divine favour we shall increase yet much more, & especially, if we have the smiles of heaven to incline y[r] Hon[rs] to grant this, our humble request, which will remove the great discouragement to sober inhabitants settling among us.

Y[r] Petitioners shall ever Pray, &c.

Farmers be allowed to be a society by themselves, destinct from ye Town Plot. [The bounds of sd society; to begin at the mouth of Beaver brook, then by a line to Doct. Hartshorne's house, thence to Scotch Cap gate, then to ye river, then by ye river to Lebanon line and by Lebanon to Shoatuck (Shetucket) river, by ye river to ye first station.]

A True Coppy of Record,

Test: R. BUSHNELL, *Clerk.*

Daniel Wicom,   Jacob Hazzen,
John Elderkin, Jun',   Joseph Edgerton,
Incres Mosely,   Christopher Huntington,
Thomas Wood,   Daniel Rockwell,
John Waterman,   John Hazen,
Thomas Hazzen,   Tho : Stoder,
Obadiah Smith,   Samuel Edgerton,
Israll Lothrup,   Joseph Kingsbery,
Joseph Kingsbery, Jun', Winslow Tracy,
Ebeneezer Johnson,   Nathaniel Badger,
Joseph Baker,   John Badger,
Joseph Downer, Jr.,   Joseph Renalls, Jun',
Joseph Downer,   Samuel Lad,
Johnathan Hartshorne, Nathaniel Lad,
Johnathan Roice,   david Lad,
Thomas Hide,   Thomas Sluman,
Thomas Hazzen,   Samuel Hide, Jur,
Benjamin Armstrong,   Joseph Ayer,
Samuel Raymond,   Joseph Ayer, Jr.,
John Armstrong,   Johnathan Lad,
John Johnson,   Sims Langly.

This petition is readily sanctioned by the legislature, and our society therefore dates its existence from October, 1716, it being the *second* society organized in the old nine miles square, and so designated till the division of the town in 1786. At first its territorial limits were quite extensive. In addition to most of the present town of Franklin, it also embraced the western half of the present town of Sprague, and the eastern part of New Concord, afterwards known as Bozrah, in all about three times its extent at the abolition of the territorial jurisdictions of ecclesiastical societies.

Measures are at once taken to put the new society into active operation. The first meeting is held November

1st; Serj. Nathaniel Rudd, Lieut. Thomas Hazen and Serj. Obadiah Smith, are chosen society committee, and Jabez Hide (by a remarkable coincidence direct ancestor of our present clerk) society clerk; it is voted to proceed to the erection of a church edifice; to call a minister, and, till the building is ready, to meet for divine worship at private dwellings. The services thus held alternate between the houses of James Birchard and Dr. David Hartshorne. Meanwhile, work upon the new edifice is pushed forward as rapidly as possible. The timber is felled upon the hill, and the frame set up near by, "down att ye walnut bush where ye path comes up ye hill," and in the locality occupied by the two following churches. The land was the gift of Joshua Abel. But with the limited means at the command of the society, progress is necessarily slow, and it is not till the next summer that the building receives its outside covering and floors; this done, the pulpit and seats of the old church at the Town Plot are procured for temporary use, and the first services held within its walls. During the warm weather up to this time, the congregation had gathered in Benjamin Peck's barn. Hungering for the living truth, they stripped off the dry husks of form, having not yet learned the faith which feeds upon external things alone. Two years after, the lower portion of the house is finished off, and in 1729 galleries are added, when the edifice, slowly erected out of scanty means by sacrifice and self-denial, can, at length, be pronounced complete.

The early gatherings in private dwellings and the unfinished church, are under the exclusive control of the society. It is not till the second Wednesday of October, 1718, one Hundred and Fifty years ago to-day, on occasion of the ordination of Rev. Henry Willes, that a church is organized as co-ordinate with the society in the management of religious affairs.* This society, therefore, is two years older than the church connected with it— not an uncommon occurrence in the early history of our State. The society supplies the more material elements which come first in point of time. Being an incorporate body, it can purchase and hold property, and is especially designed to provide a place for public worship and to defray the cost of maintaining the gospel ordinances therein, matters which the church, a body unrecognized at law, cannot well arrange, though they are of the first importance. Naturally, then, the organization of a society is the first step, and frequently, in primitive days, the church was not gathered till long afterward; the society maintained all the ordinances except the communion and baptism, for which the people had to resort to some neighboring church. Thus, for instance, in Lyme the society ranked some thirty years prior to the church.

But other concerns besides the building of a meeting

---

* We subjoin the following petition extracted from the Archives of Connecticut.

To the Honble Gurdon Saltonstall, Governr in and over his Mats colloney of Connecticut in New England, And . . . . The Honble the councill and the Representatives in General Court Assembled at Hartford this eighth of May, 1715.

The Humble Petition of the Inhabitants of that Part of Norwich which is called or . . . . known by the name of West Farmers within the Colloncy of Connecticut Aforesaid, Humbly Sheweth.

That whereas this Honble Court at their Session at New Haven In ye month of October In ye year 1716, In answer to ye petition, To us sd Inhabitants Did Grant us Liberty to be a society by ourselves, which Petition or Liberty being granted, we have Invited The Revnd Mr. Henry Willes to preach ye gospel Amongst us; who having been with us some time on probation—we have now mutually agreed with him In order to settlement Amongst us In the work of The Ministry.

Signed in ye behalf of ye Society,

DAVID HARTSHORNE, THOMAS SLUMAN.

} Wherefore we, your most Humble Petitioners, crave and earnestly desire this Honble Court's Approbation And Consent to proceed to ordination, and an allowance to Imbody ourselves Into Church Estate.

house and engagement of a pastor demand immediate
attention. In former days the interests of education were
entrusted to the care of the different societies, and with
the happiest results. The same conscientious fidelity to
duty which impelled our fathers to maintain the ordinances
of religion at any sacrifice, impelled them also to stud the
land with school houses, that an intelligent faith might be
within grasp of all, and that the state might be planted on
the sure foundation of popular education. One of the
first acts of the society relates to a society school. This
school is located upon Meeting House hill and kept open
six months of the year. A portion of the cost is defrayed
by the state, but the society also contributes freely, voting
annually to this object twenty-five or thirty pounds. Yet
the best endeavors could provide the youth of that day
with no royal road to learning. However able the instructor, or diligent the scholar, the want of cheap and
systematic text books was a formidable barrier to high
attainment. Not infrequently the teacher owned the
only arithmetic or grammar to be found in the school.
In this society the distant scholars encountered the
additional obstacle of a walk of three or four miles morning and night. This inconvenience led, in 1727, to the
division of the society into four school districts; Portipaug, Upper Windham road, Lower Windham road and
Lebanon road. But the population was too scanty for the
maintenance of separate schools, and the division remained inoperative till, in 1729, this difficulty was curiously
obviated by a school which traveled from district to district, keeping six weeks in each. This migratory school
proved a complete success. All were delighted with it,
and for many seasons the pedagogue continued his itinerant sway.

Still other matters press upon the attention from the

very outset, some of them trivial in themselves, though highly important as illustrations of the extensive functions of the early societies. Thus, our own society had delegated to it additional powers which resembled those of our present town government. While it could impose taxes upon the entire community and had control of schools, its records show that it also engaged in such civil affairs as the laying out of highways, and even went so far as to build a public pound. Burying grounds were also under its charge, and the society early took care to provide a suitable cemetery. The spot selected was upon "the playne"* where Benjamin Peck had previously buried a daughter. This ground, twice afterward enlarged, is the one in use at the present day. For many years it was the only regular cemetery in the society, though a few graves were dug, at an early day, upon a sandy knoll jutting into the Great Pine Swamp, and now commonly called the Indian Burying Ground.

All in all, for the first few years the young society flourished finely. The tide of prosperity, however, could not flow on forever, and in 1734 the current changes. That year the General Assembly permit the people of New Concord (the western part of the society) to procure preaching by themselves, and two years later incorporate them into a distinct society. Deprived thereby of a fifth of her territory, the parent society resists the movement vigorously, and, could she have foreseen the endless troubles destined to follow in its train, would, doubtless, have staked her all upon the issue; for this secession proved the first cause of twenty years of the most turbulent commotion, and of a second more vital change. The society had, by this time, outgrown the first church, which

---

* The Plain was then usually called "Birchard's Plain."

was probably a rude affair, and were nearly agreed upon
the propriety of building a new one, when the withdrawal
of New Concord gave an unexpected turn to the matter.
Before her withdrawal the church had stood in the exact
center of the society, but now it was thrown a mile to one
side, and this trifling change proved sufficient to develop
a bitter controversy as to the location of the new church,
and to arouse an Ætna of feeling which twenty years were
powerless to assauge. About half of the society contend
for the old location, while the other half strenuously maintain that the new building ought to stand farther east, in
the real center. It is voted to build upon the old spot,
rescinded, voted again, and then, as a temporary compromise, to repair and enlarge the present building ; but
this proposition shares the fate of the rest, and at the end
of several years of constant agitation, the society finds
itself at a perfect standstill. Finally, as the only egress,
a majority petition the General Assembly for a committee
to come and settle the disputed point. The committee
sent in response to this petition, visit West Farms in the
fall of 1741, spend two days in hearing the opposing
parties, and report : " (1), That it is necessary that a new
meeting house should be erected in said society ; (2), that
it will best accommodate the greater part of the people
there, and tend most to peace to have the same built on
the hill where the old meeting house stands, and as follows,
viz.: that the south-westerly corner be laid about twenty
feet west of an old chestnut stub yt is about forty feet from
the southwest corner of the old meeting house, and to extend
toward ye old meeting house in ye length as far as may be
convenient, and to the northward of sd stump in ye
width." This report meets the approval of the legislature,
and the society is directed to build upon the spot selected.

Though the disputed points have now been authorita-

tively settled, the troubles are by no means at an end.
Old jealousies and animosities still lurk behind, and render
the erection of the new edifice as difficult as was the selection of the spot on which it should stand. The sounding board used to bear in bold, black figures, the date of
1745, but the reports of the clerk to the General Assembly
show that it was not completed till after 1747.

Not a few of the audience will readily recall this second
church, with its immense sounding board, the wonder of
boyish days, its double row of high backed pews running
around the sides, and enclosing in the center two tiers of
slips, between which ran the broad main aisle, leading up
to the Deacons' Seat, and the little antique pulpit, cush-
ioned with gray and hung round with long, black tassels,
that used to sway in the summer wind like a pall. In the
center were seated the aged people, husbands and wives
on opposite sides, while the younger families gathered in
the surrounding pews, and the young unmarried people
ranged themselves in pert, prim rows in either gallery,
the men on the right and the women on the left. Behind
these were the wall pews of the galleries, so lofty that
their chance occupants seemed, as it were, suspended in
huge boxes from the ceiling. Conspicuous in front was
the Deacons' Seat, and high above it the pulpit, from
which for many years successive pastors had proclaimed
the word of life. All was plain, simple, and tinged, perhaps, with a sombre air. The church was plain, the
people were plain, and the message of the preacher fell with
a plain earnestness that went direct to every heart. Alto-
gether, it was a fair type of the puritan congregation as it
had earlier existed over all New England, and yet a congregation how worthy of imitation in their devout
attention, and their religious zeal, that worked like leaven
through the entire community, bringing every man, woman

and child unto the house of God, and fairly realizing the words of ancient writ, " *All* the people praised the Lord."

But hark, the roll of a drum announces the approaching hour of worship, and along the converging roads the people may be seen climbing to the sanctuary. From the South, the Hydes, Hartshornes, Rudds and Rogerses; from the East, the Barkers, Fillmores, Ayreses, Ladds, Elderkins, Birchards, Armstrongs and Pembers ; from the North, the Kingsburys, Edgertons, Badgers, Downers, Gagers, Barstows and Tracys ; from the West, the Huntingtons, Johnsons, Slumans, Roods, Lathrops, Crockers, Pettises, Tracys and Masons are drawing near. The men on horseback with their wives behind them, the children and poorer people on foot, slowly and thoughtfully are wending their way to the house of God. As they approach, glance at them. The men are arrayed in powdered wigs, ruffled shirts, elaborately embroidered waistcoats with white lappels, knee breeches, silk stockings and silver buckled shoes. Their wives, with hair piled up " in curls on curls before and mounted to a formidable tower " appear entirely in garments of domestic fabrication, cut in a manner betokening an eye in their wearers for the prevailing fashion, which certainly will compare favorably in capriciousness with post-colonial days. Entering, in either corner is posted a tything man, with long slender rod in hand, to preserve order, while the deacons are already standing in their conspicuous pew. But see, the drum has ceased its roll, and the pastor approaches across the green, and with slow and measured step enters the church. Instantly all noise is hushed, the deacons quietly and reverently take their seats, the tything men lay aside their rods, and the congregation waits in order for the opening of the service. Rev. Mr. Willes calls out the number of a Hymn and reads :—

> " Hierusalem, my happy home !
>   When shall I come to thee !
>   When shall my sorrowes have an end,
>   Thy joyes when shall I see? "

Immediately Deacon Kingsbury, (as books were not abundant at that day), "deacons off" the line. Artemus Downer, the schoolmaster, strikes up some favorite tune, and the entire congregation, young and old, perhaps with not the best of harmony, but yet with earnest tones, respond—

> " Hierusalem, my happy home !
>   When shall I come to thee ! "

The hymn concluded, the people rise and stand during the prayer that follows. This finished, they resume their seats, the pastor sets up his hour glass, announces his text, and reads on from a cramped and dingy manuscript till the sands are run, to the great edification of his hearers, who listen with unabstracted gaze, save when the tything man, Judah Smith, comes up the aisle to reprove Talatha Morgan for "laughing and playing."* A short prayer

---

* To Eben' Hartshorne, of Norwich, in New London County, one of his Majesty's Justices of the peace for sd county, comes Judah Smith of sd Norwich, one of the Tything men chosen by ye sd Town of Norwich for ye west Society in said Norwich, and Informs and upon oath presents that Talatha Morgan of sd Norwich, single woman, Did on ye 24th day of February last, it being ye Sabbath or Lord's day, prophane sd Lord's day in ye meeting house in ye west society in ye time of ye forenoon service on sd day by her Rude and Indecent Behaviour in Laughing and playing in ye time of sd service, which Doings of ye sd Talatha is against ye peace of our Sovereign Lord, the King, his Crown and Dignity, and contrary to the Statute in such case made and provided. Dated at Norwich, ye 19th Day of April, A. D. 1747, and in ye 20th year of his Majesty's Reign.

Take for evidences, Judah Smith, Tything Man, Cibel Waterman ye wife of Eben' Waterman, Jun' , and Judah Smith. Both of sd Norwich.

1747. April 28, the above named Talatha Morgan appeared personally and pleaded guilty to ye above presentment, and sentenced to pay a fine £0, 3, 0, and £0, 1, 0, cost for her above transgression, by me ye above named Justice. ———which fine and cost is paid.

follows the sermon, ending in the benediction, the closing
word of which has barely fallen from the pastor's lips,
when, from his corner, the tything man cries in sharp,
quick tones, "James Elderkin and Betty Waterman intend
marriage;" and so the congregation break up, and wend
their way homeward, to meditate upon the lessons of the
sermon, though some, perhaps, to wonder why and when
Miss Betty Waterman is to become Mrs. James Elderkin.

And here we will linger a moment over a custom long
since abandoned ; the custom of seating the church. In
early times, the expenses of the society were met by a
direct tax, instead of a levy on the pews and slips, and
these were consequently free. But to preserve the gravity
and decorum of the assembly, to secure the nearer and
conspicuous seats for aged listeners, and to prevent assur-
ance from pushing aside honest worth, a committee was
annually appointed to assign permanent seats to the congregation, in accordance with their ideas of propriety,
though in conformity to the general rule of "age and
estate." This office of virtually pronouncing upon the
worth and respectability of the different members of the
community was no enviable one, and many were the
jealousies enkindled by it, not infrequently resulting in several seatings of the church before a satisfactory one could
be obtained. It is related that a certain worthy individual,
entering the society under unfavorable prejudices, was
assigned an obscure seat in a remote corner, and, that
though he afterwards proved a most valuable acquisition
to the society, he always clung to his humble seat, to the
great discomfiture of the committee who had put so low
an estimate upon his worth.

Very fortunately, a number of the reports of these
committees have been preserved, and we are thereby

furnished with the exact arrangement of the congrega-
tions of a century ago. These seatings also show us, seated
side by side, year after year, the immediate ancestors of
such a galaxy of distinguished men as probably few other
country towns in the land can boast of as her own. Here
were habitually seated the ancestors of Hon. Millard
Fillmore, late President of the United States; the father
and grandfather of Hon. Uriah Tracy, United States
Senator from Connecticut and President of the Senate;
the ancestors of Hon. L. F. S. Foster, United States
Senator from Connecticut and also President of the
Senate; of Hon. Jeremiah Mason, United States Senator
from New Hampshire; of the Hon. Abel Huntington,
Uri Tracy, Phineas L. Tracy and Albert H. Tracy, mem-
bers of Congress from the State of New York; of Hon.
Alfred P. Edgerton, member of Congress from Indiana;
of Hon. John Tracy, Lieut. Governor of New York; of
Hon. Ephraim H. Hyde, present Lieut. Governor of
Connecticut; of Rev. Azel Backus, Pres't of Hamilton
college; of Rev. Charles Backus, Professor of Divinity in
Yale college; and of several other distinguished members
of the clerical profession, as well as of many more who have
attained honorable eminence in the different walks of life.
These persons were generally to the manor born, but when
otherwise, their ancestral homes can all be pointed within
our territorial limits and most of them have blood relatives
in our midst.

It is a favorite theme of congratulation among the sons
of Connecticut, that their state has given birth to so many
of the men who have been prominent in the history of the
nation; and surely, no town of our extent, in this grand
old state of Connecticut, can furnish a prouder list than
our own. Our society, then, may well rejoice that she
has helped to form the characters of men who have been

so potent in moulding our country's destiny, and that through them her humble influence has been felt throughout the length and breadth of the land.

We have already stated that the action of the committee sent out by the General Assembly in 1741, failed to quiet the troubled elements of the society. The feelings and convictions of the contending parties were too firm to be easily yielded, and the eastern party, believing as they did, that their rights had been wholly ignored, became even more dicontented than before. The next year, 1742, a large number of memorialists, headed by John Durkee and Jacob Hyde, petition the General Assembly, saying that the church now being erected by the Assembly's order, is unjustly located on one side of the society, at an unreasonable distance from their homes, and that the inconvenience of journeying thither to church will be far greater than the burthen of maintaining a separate organization, and praying, therefore, for liberty to withdraw and form a separate society. The Assembly, unwilling to reflect upon the action of its committee, negative the petition. Nothing daunted, two years after, the same memorialists prefer the same petition, and again fail. Two petitions sent in in 1745 from the north-eastern and south-eastern parts of the society, meet a similar fate. But the popular mind is too deeply roused to be disheartened by these continued rebuffs, and the next year sixty voters renew the petition, and this time so far prevail that Jonathan Trumble, John Ledyard and Christopher Avery are sent out to West Farms to adjust their difficulties. The efforts of this committee prove ineffectual, though after their visit the controversy takes an unexpected turn. Thomas Dennison, an itinerant preacher, had entered the society some time before, and in the prevailing distraction gathered a goodly number of disciples. What his par-

ticular tenets were, is uncertain, but it is evident that he added fresh fuel to the strife, and contributed in no small degree to the change which it assumed soon after his arrival. It seems that Rev. Henry Willes stood upon the Cambridge Platform of 1608, in which we may presume he received the tacit support of the society, as no opposition to his views had ever appeared. Of a sudden, however, we find half of the society in arms against their pastor for his adhesion to the Cambridge Platform, and the other half as zealous in his support. The old proposition for a division, which doubtless lay at the bottom of this theological war, now starts up in a new form. In 1748 the General Assembly is petitioned to divide West Farms into two societies, one to be planted on the Cambridge, the other on the Saybrook Platform. In response to this novel memorial, a committee is sent out, who recommend no change. Four years later, another committee is sent out for the same object, and with the same result. The society had now for fifteen years been engaged in uninterrupted strife, during which the arbitration of the legislature had been continually invoked, but always with unsatisfactory results, and both parties wisely concluded that their troubles, if ever settled, must be settled by themselves and not by the interference of a higher power. Accordingly, we find no more petitions to the General Assembly. Yet the bitterness and ill will, the discord and dissension, are in no wise at an end. For a while the seceders, being in the minority, accomplish no visible result. But after a few years the majority apparently become convinced that separation alone can restore peace and tranquillity, and in March, 1758, consent to the formation of a new society, provided a boundary line and the number of inhabitants to be set off, can be agreed upon. Such is the testy temper, however, that it is as difficult to

3

agree upon the boundary line as it has been upon separation, and it is not till 1761 that this point can be
arranged, when, upon the 23d of March, a line is at length
fixed upon.* These proceedings receive the ready sanc-
tion of the legislature, and the new society is incorporated
as the Norwich Eighth or Portipaug society.

Thus, after twenty years of constant strife, at length
dawned peace. These years may be called, emphatically,
the stormy period in the history of our society. Before,
as after, its proceedings were invariably marked by harmony and unanimity, but during the interval there was a
display of feeling unparalleled for bitterness and persistency in the ecclesiastical annals of Connecticut. The
issue was doubtless best for all concerned, for the existing
breach was too wide to be ever healed. Yet the loss to
our society in territory and numbers was a serious one.
New Concord and the Eighth Society combined, stripped
her of over half of her territory, and quite half of her
grand list.

* "The dividing line shall be as follows; to begin in the Dividing Line
between the first society in sd Norwich and sd west society at such a place
that to run to the Grist Mill of Mr. Timothy Ayer, will pass near the south
side of the Dwelling House of David Ladd, then from sd Grist Mill to the
Dwelling House of Mr John Squire in sd society, then the same course to sd
Norwich Town Line." Petition to the Legislature.

The signers of this petition were :—

Joseph Bingham,	Simon Abel,	Ezekiel Ladd,
John Fillmore,	Saml Kingsley,	Joseph Ayer,
Joseph Tenney,	Andrew French,	John Barker,
Joseph Rudd,	Saml Ladd, Junr,	Jacob Hide, Jr.,
Joseph Hide,	Jeremiah Armstrong,	John Squire,
Saml Badger,	Alpheus Abell,	Abner Ladd,
Daniel Ladd,	Wm. Brett,	Barnabus Lothrup,
Jabez Rous,	Joseph Ayre, Jr.,	Timothy Ayer,
Benajah Sabin,	Johnathan Pitcher,	Richard Haskin,
James Elderkin,	Benja Armstrong,	Josiah Wood,
Saml Raymond,	Simon Chapman,	Leander Lothrup,
Eliphalet Fox,	Thomas Hazen,	Simon Peck,
Asa Armstrong,	John Kingsley,	Daniel Story,
David Lad,	Ephraim Brett.	

Scarcely are domestic troubles at an end, when public calamities break upon the land, and the men of our society are called upon to shoulder arms. Through the French war and the long and toilsome Revolution that followed, they shrank not from their share of the heavy burthens. As Connecticut was first among the states in her contributions of men and money, as Norwich was second to no town in Connecticut, so West Farms, an integral portion of the old town of Norwich, met manfully the duties of those trying days. Having then no political existence, her deeds were swallowed up in those of the larger community to which she was attached, and hence receive little mention in the local histories. Her volunteers marched forth as Norwich volunteers; as citizens of Norwich, her inhabitants met the heavy levies which the necessities of the time so often imposed. Why may we not, then, also claim a share in the laurels which Norwich won? But we may also point with pride to particular individuals. Our society can boast of having furnished, perhaps, the only chaplain, Rev. John Ellis, who remained in the war from its beginning to its close. Mr. Ellis hastened to join the army at Roxbury, in the fall of 1775, and faithfully followed it through all its vicissitudes, especially doing much to cheer the drooping spirits of his comrades during the long and gloomy winter at Valley Forge. Here Lieut. Jacob Kingsbury began his long and honorable military career, serving with distinction during the entire seven years of the war. Captains Asa Hartshorne, Ebenezer Hartshorne and Joshua Barker were also in the army for different periods, while upon the water, West Farms was well represented by the exploits of Captain James Hyde. Dr. Luther Waterman was attached as surgeon to the forces under Colonel Knowlton in the campaign of 1776.

The close of the Revolution left the society in a greatly embarrassed condition. During its progress she had contributed freely of her men and means, entering into the contest with such absorbing enthusiasm as left no room for the consideration of private or local interests, and at its close she found herself utterly prostrated, her school houses decayed, the education of her sons neglected, (says Dr. Nott, "so far as I can recollect, there was not a man that pretended to understand grammar or geography,") her farms run to weeds, and her people heavily loaded with debt. At no time in her history had her prospects been more wretched. A fortunate concurrence of circumstances, however, soon placed her upon her feet, and restored her wonted prosperity. In 1782, Rev. Samuel Nott, at the unanimous request of both church and society, was settled as their pastor. Mr. Nott was a wise, judicious man, eminently fitted to harmonize any discordant feeling which might exist, and fitted by his energy to infuse fresh life into the prevailing stagnation. Another happy event was the incorporation of the West and Eighth societies as a separate town, which severed the connection of West Farms with Norwich, and ensured a more efficient management of local affairs than they had before received. Perhaps too much praise cannot be bestowed upon the efforts of Rev. Mr. Nott to ameliorate the condition of his people. Scrupulously faithful in the discharge of pastoral duties, he also did a vast deal toward the education of the younger members of his parish, affording them opportunities of which they gladly availed themselves. During his long ministry more than forty young men were fitted for college under his care, twenty of them belonging to this town, and "between two and three hundred gentlemen, ladies or children" were educated in whole or in part.* As an instructor, Dr. Nott was popular and singularly successful, and Franklin became the place where quite a galaxy of distinguished men received their education. Here were gathered under his charge at different times, Dr. Eliphalet Nott, President of Union college, the brilliant but erratic General Wm. Eaton, Lieut. Gov. Tracy, of New York, and many others who have since achieved distinguished success in the different walks of life. Though moving in a humble sphere, Dr. Nott, by means of his teachings and wholesome counsels, wielded a power for good in the land which it has been the privilege of few to surpass. It was mainly due to his influence that the Franklin Library was established, in 1794, an institution which flourished for forty years and furnished, for the times, a good collection of miscellaneous works. Under these different salutary influences the society rapidly retrieved her lost ground, and by the beginning of the present century was, perhaps, as flourishing as ever.

During the present century the society has witnessed few changes. At its commencement she had attained a settled state, and since then her affairs have flowed on smoothly and prosperously, but so quietly that few marked events arrest the attention. One after another, of her extended civil powers have dropped from her grasp, so that she is now a purely voluntary organization, but the loss is more than compensated by the steadily increasing prosperity of her community, and we may safely say that her condition was never more hopeful than to-day. The liberality of former members and friends has also helped to to build up her walls, and we cannot pass on without a tribute to their memory. Deacon Dyer McCall died May

---

* Dr. Nott's Half Century Sermon.

19th, 1838, crowning a life of benevolence by bequeathing the bulk of his fortune to various charitable organizations, of which this society was the recipient of one quarter, a sum amounting to Two Thousand dollars. Eleven years later his wife, Lucy, dying, added a similar sum to the fund of the society.* In 1838, also, Miss Velina Sanford bequeathed her entire estate to the society, thereby adding another thousand to its funds. In 1863, Ezra Chappel, Esq., of New London, a gentleman of whole-souled benevolence, generously stayed our hands in a time of difficulty by contributing Fifteen Hundred dollars for building purposes. In this connection we cannot omit to mention David Edgerton who died in 1768, leaving all his real estate forever to be improved for schooling youth in this society to the latest generation. Mr. Edgerton was a strong pillar of the society in his own day, and the rich blessings flowing from his gift are a proud monument to the wisdom and foresight of the giver. Joshua Abel was another donor to the society, he having given the ground on which our first three churches stood. Let us ever hold in grateful remembrance the memory of these different benefactors, the fruits of whose benevolence we enjoy to-day, and whose charity, the noblest of all human qualities, certainly entitles them to the highest place in our calendar.

But the different churches afford the surest landmarks for denoting the successive epochs of our history. The second church, erected in 1745, battled from its bleak eminence with storms and winds for nearly a century, but finally had to yield, and, in 1836, gave way to a more modern structure, located midway between the places of

---

* This lady also made a small bequest for the support of the poor of the church.

the first and second churches. This third church had barely
attained a quarter of the age of its predecessor, when in
its turn it had to make way for the fourth church, the one
in which we are at present assembled, and which was
erected in 1863, a short distance below the location of the
other churches. The same year the society was enabled,
by the generosity of the late Edward Chappel of New
London, (to whom allusion has already been made), a christian gentleman of unmeasured benevolence, and grandfather of our present pastor, to erect a parsonage. This
parsonage affords convenient data for locating our first
three churches. The second church appears to have
stood upon the exact location of the parsonage, the first
church immediately East, and the third church immediately West.

We have thus followed the history of this community
from the time when the first settlers pitched their tents in
these valleys, down through two centuries to the present
day. We have seen the solitude of the wilderness broken
by the first log cabin, we have seen the forests gradually
recede before the advance of civilization, and the rugged
wildness of nature slowly exchanged for a more peaceful beauty, till at length our hills have been crowned with
the ameliorations of progress, our valleys filled with the
hum of industry, and the echoes of the war whoop
drowned in the shriek of the locomotive and the clatter
of machinery.

Through all these mighty changes, this society has
been working potently for good. Through all these
years she has kept a beacon fire alive upon this hill top,
and drawn up hither generation after generation, to worship God. By the inspiration of her presence, she has
made this community ever a virtuous, Heaven-fearing
people, and rendered those who have gone forth from

here valiant to do battle for the right. Surely, then, her part has been well done. Within her own sphere she has faithfully discharged her duties, and who shall measure her influence through those sons reared up and sent forth to fill exalted stations in other and wider spheres. Let us see to it that she declines not in our hands.

———•♦•———

NOTE A.

INDIAN DEED OF NORWICH.

Deed from Onkos, and his sons Oneco and Attawanhood, Sachems of
Mohegan, of a tract of Land nine miles square, for the settlement of
the town of Norwich. Anno Domini 1659.

As this Deed covers every foot of territory now within the limits of
the town of Franklin, and as portions of this ancient domain have
never been alienated, but are still in the occupancy of the descendants of
the original Proprietors, it has been deemed proper to insert it in this
place.

DEED.

Know All men that Onkos, Owaneco and Attawanhood, Sachems of
Mohegan, have bargained, sold and passed over, and doe by these
presents, bargain, sell and pass over unto the Towne and Inhabitants of
Norwich, nine miles square of lands, lyeing and being at Moheagen and
the partes thereunto adjoyning, with all ponds, rivers, woods, quarries,
mines with all Royalties, privileges and appurtenances thereunto belonging, to them the sayd Inhabitants of Norwich, their heirs and successors
forever—the sayd lands are to be bounded as followeth, (viz.,) to the
southward on the west side (of) the Great River commonly called Mon-
heag River, ye line is to begin at the Brooke falling into the head of
Trading Cove, and soe to run west norwest seven miles;—from thence
the line is to run nor-noreast nine miles; and on the east side of the
foresayd River to the southward, the line is to joyne with New-London
Bounds as it is now laid out and soe to run east Two miles from the
foresayd River, and so from thence the line is to Run nor-noreast nine
miles, and from thence to Run nor-norwest nine miles to meet the
western line. In consideration whereof the sayd Onkos, Owaneco, and
Attawanhood doe acknowledg to have received of the parties aforesayd,
the full (and juste) sum of seventy pounds, and doe promise and engage

ourselves, heirs and successors, to warrant the sayd Bargain and sale to the aforesayd parties, their heirs and successors and them to defend from all ciaimes or molestations from any whatsoever. In witness whereof wee have hereunto set our hands this sixth day of June, Anno 1659.

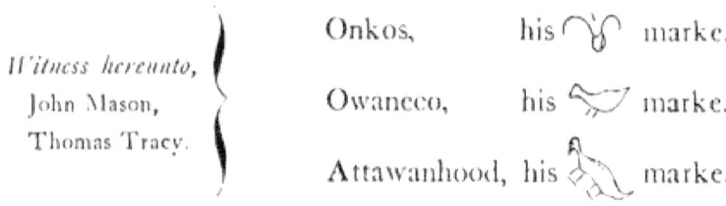

Witness hereunto,
John Mason,
Thomas Tracy.

Onkos, his marke.

Owaneco, his marke.

Attawanhood, his marke.

(This Deed is Recorded in the Country Booke, August 20th, 1663: as Atteste,

JOHN ALLYN, *Sec'y.*)

Note B.

INDIAN NAMES.

Almost the only enduring memorials of the Aborigines are the few geographical names which survived their decay, and which still remain, constantly reminding us that our streams and hills were once the haunts of a different race of men. Too often these names fall meaningless upon the ear, charming us by their mellifluence but wholly unintelligible. Yet we may be sure that they were primarily significant, and in many cases, like so much else in Indian thought, the products of bright fancies, so that, could we once arrive at their hidden meaning, its poetry would often prove delightful and offer pleasant glimpses into that form of society of which they are the only remnants.

But the difficulties in the way are very great. The early scribes wrote Indian as lawlessly as they wrote English, and unquestionably our pronunciation of many names of places is very different from the Indian pronunciation. They are clipped at one end or both,—anglicized or euphonized—until their identity is sometimes quite lost. To decipher the meaning of confused words in a dead and but imperfectly recorded language is surely no easy or certain task. Thus premising, we offer the following suggestions upon the Indian Names in this vicinity.*

---

* For these suggestions the writer is indebted to Hon. J. Hammond Trumbull, of Hartford, a gentleman who has given much time and talent to the study of the Indian language, and who is our best authority in all questions pertaining to it.

1. Shetucket. The termination shows this to be the name of a place, not of the river. In the old records it is sometimes written *Showtackett* (Conn. Col. Records, iii, 479) and *Showattukket*. In Owaneco's Reservation, (1669), "*Shawtuck* river" is named. *Shawtuck—et* is '*on*' or '*near*' the *Shawtuck*. *Tuk* signifies '*river*.' The first syllable, *Shaw* or *She*, means either '*three*' or '*between*.' It is impossible to say which; for the form is a corrupt one,—and the two words have in Indian (as in many other languages) the same radical. *Shetucket* [*She—tuck—et*) signifies "at the three rivers," (the place of the three rivers), or "at the between rivers" (the place between rivers); more probably the latter. Either name would be appropriate, as the reader will perceive.

Roger Williams mentions the Wunna*showatuck*-oogs, who lived at Wunna*showatuck*-gut or, as elsewhere written, *showatuck*-gut. These were "the furthermost Nipnet men," and lived, probably, among the rivers, or "between the rivers," north of the Massachusetts line. Shetucket is with little doubt another form of the same name, in its contract form.

2. Yantic. Old forms, *Yantuck*, *Yontahguc* and (in record of Uncas's deed) *Yontacke*. We incline to derive it from *yan*, 'four' and *tuk*, 'river'; but there is nearly an equal probability that it is from *Yoĭë*, on, or 'at that side'; the river [which comes in] at that side, [or, according to the locus of the speaker, at *this* side] of the main river; i. e., 'The river from one side,' or *lateral tributary*. The mode of entrance of this stream into the Thames might very naturally suggest this name.

3. Susquetomscot. Otherwise, *Sukskotumskot*. The two last syllables, *omscot*, mean, certainly, 'at the rock,'—but the prefix, *susquet*, is doubtful. This prefix qualifies *ompsk* (=*omsc*,) 'rock.' For example, soggohtunkan-ompsk, the *flint* rock ; tomheganompsk, the *axe* rock (or rock from which tomahawks were made,) &c. But we cannot fix confidently the meaning of *susquet* or *sukskot*. The Susquetomscot is our wildest and rockiest stream, and it would be highly interesting to know from what circumstance connected with its rockiness it drew its name. We naturally infer that the name is in some way connected with the rocky gorge near the Peck Hollow Railroad Station.

4. Pootapaug or Pautipaug. This name was also given to a part of, or place in, what is now Essex,—and is written *Pauta-*, *Porti-* and *Petti- -paug*, *-pog*, and *-pawg*. Eliot has almost the exact word, *pootuppog*

and *pootuppag*, for 'a bay,' in Joshua xv : 2, 5. The primary significa-
tion seems to be, a recess or 'corner' of water. *Poot sai* means a corner, i. e., interior, not salient ; the space included. Literally, *pootup-
paug*, which Eliot translates ' bay,' signifies ' corner-water,' nearly equiv-
alent perhaps to our word 'cove.' In Essex this name is appropriate,
but why it should have been attached to any portion of Franklin is
difficult to see.

Note C.

The following is a complete list of the Thirty-five Original Proprietors who settled Norwich in 1660.

These names necessarily occur so often under note D, that a published list will doubtless be found convenient for reference. When not
prefixed by an asterisk, they were surviving in January, in the year
1700.

Rev. James Fitch, the first minister of
    Norwich,
*Major John Mason, afterwards Lt. Gov.
    of Connecticut,
Deacon Thomas Adgate,
Lieut. William Backus, Jr.,
*Stephen Backus, brother of Wm., Jr.,
    above,
*John Baldwin,
*John Birchard,
*Thomas Bliss,
Morgan Bowers,
*Richard Edgerton,
*Francis Griswold,
*Christopher Huntington,
Deacon Simon Huntington, brother of
    Christopher, above,
*William Hyde,
*Samuel Hyde, son of William, above,
Lieut. Thomas Leffingwell,
*Doctor John Olmstead,
John Post, son-in-law of Wm. Hyde,
Thomas Post,
John Reynolds,
*Lieut. Thomas Tracy,
*Thomas Bingham, a minor in 1660,
*Stephen Gifford, a minor in 1660,
*Thomas Howard, a minor in 1660,
John Tracy, a minor in 1660, son of Lt.
    Thomas Tracy,
*Josiah Reed, a minor in 1660.

These settlers came
from Saybrook and East
Saybrook (now Lyme),
to Norwich, Anno Dom-
ini 1660

*Robert Allyn,
*Deacon Hugh Calkins,
*John Calkins, son of Dea. Hugh, above,
*Jonathan Royce, son-in-law of Dea. Hugh
    Calkins,
*John Gager,
*John Pease,
*Nehemiah Smith.

These settlers came from New London to Norwich, Anno Domini 1660.

*John Bradford,
*Ensign Thomas Waterman, a minor in
    1660.

These settlers came from Marshfield, Mass., to Norwich, Anno Domini 1660.

NOTE D.

Brief notices of the principal original settlers of West Farms, now Franklin.

Abell, Joshua, came hither from Dedham, Mass., before 1670. He settled in the valley east of Meeting House hill, and became a very considerable land holder. His dwelling was near the present residence of Henry W. Kingsley, but upon the opposite side of the highway. The lot upon which the first Meeting House was erected, and which is now connected with the parsonage, was a gift from him to the society. He married Mehetabel, a daughter of Nehemiah Smith, one of the original Thirty-Five (35) Proprietors of Norwich. He had six daughters, several of whom were married to first comers. He died March 17th, 1724, in the 77th year of his age. He left no son. His brothers Caleb and Benjamin came to the Colony with him, but settled in other parts of Norwich.

Armstrong, Benjamin, son of Jonathan of Westerly, R. I., became a settler in 1682. His dwelling was nearly opposite to the entrance to the lane leading to the residence of Geo. E. Starkweather. He died Jan. 10th, 1717–18, leaving sons Benjamin, John, Joseph and Stephen.

John Armstrong married, in 1710, Anne Worth and remained upon the paternal homestead, where he had twelve children. His descendants have been numerous and most of the families in the vicinity bearing the name are of his line. He was often entrusted with office in the Society which he always worthily filled. He died in 1748.

Arnold, John, was a land holder both by grant and purchase, as early as 1683. After a long occupancy he finally alienated his estate and removed to Windham. The " Arnold Place" afterwards became the homestead of Rev. Henry Willes. It is now occupied by Dr. Stephen Sweet.

Ayer, John, born in England, was brought to this country while an infant, in 1630, by his parents, who located at Haverhill, Mass. He married, May 5, 1646, Sarah Williams, of Haverhill, and had by her five children. He married for second wife, at Haverhill, March 26, 1663, Mary Moodam, by whom he had one child. Soon after his second marriage he became involved in serious personal difficulties with the Massachusetts Indians, and to save his life moved secretly and alone to West Farms. The exact year of his arrival is uncertain, but without doubt it was as early as 1665, and he may be safely called the first white settler of the town. His location was Ayer's Gap. Here he lived by himself for many years, pursuing his favorite vocation of hunting and trapping with great success. It is said that in the chase and all the mysteries of woodcraft, his skill and sagacity fully equalled that of the Indians, between whom and himself there was, indeed, a constant rivalry, which not infrequently ripened into open warfare. Many are the traditions of this strange man, lingering around the scenes of his life, and his adventures with Indians and wild beasts still form the theme of numerous stories related with zest around the winter's fire. These stories, without exception, delineate him as a man of striking eccentricities, but withal, of great endurance, heroic fortitude and a rare presence of mind that never forsook him in time of danger.

Rattlesnakes were the only foes whom John Ayer feared. These swarmed into his cabin in such numbers from the surrounding ledges, that he was almost in despair, and thought of abandoning the place. But a friend in Massachusetts urged him first to try the efficiency of hogs in destroying the reptiles. Accordingly, Ayer procured several hogs from the nearest settlement, and these soon effectually rid his premises of his troublesome visitors.

His son Joseph, born at Haverhill, March 16, 1658, married, Nov. 24, 1686, Sarah Corliss, of Haverhill, where he continued till about the year 1700, when he removed to West Farms to reside with his father, now well stricken in years, bringing with him his youngest two sons, Joseph and Timothy. The descendants of Mr. Ayer still remain in Franklin.

Backus, Lieut. William, Jr., the Proprietor, had sons William, John, Joseph and Nathaniel.

Nathaniel Backus married Elizabeth Tracy and settled at West Farms.

His dwelling was where Col. T. G. Kingsley now resides. Jabez, their fourth child, born in Aug. 1712, married Eunice Kingsbury and remained upon the paternal homestead. He was the father of Rev. Charles Backus, D. D., the acute and able theologian. The Rev. Azel Backus, D. D., first President of Hamilton College, also descended from him through his eldest son Jabez, being his grandson.

Badger, John, came early to West Farms from Newbury, Mass. His place was on Center Hill on the old road leading north from the residence of the late Backus Smith. He had a son, Samuel, but the name has long been extinct in the town. For site of dwelling see accompanying map.

Barstow, Job, a son of John, of Scituate, Mass, was born March 8, 1679. He came hither early in life and settled where Joseph I. Hyde now resides. This place had previously been in the occupancy of Joseph Reynolds. He married Rebecca, a daughter of Joseph Bushnell, and had sons Jonathan, Ebenezer and Get-once, and daughter Jerusha. His name often appears upon the records of the Society in honorable relations.

Bingham, Dea. Thomas, an original Proprietor of Norwich in 1660, and the common ancestor of the Connecticut families of the name, was the son of Thomas and Mary Bingham, of Sheffield, England, and was born about 1642. He married Mary Rudd and became an early resident of Windham. His son, Thomas, born December 11, 1667, married Hannah Backus and succeeded to the privileges of his father as a proprietor in Norwich. Their eldest son Thomas, of the third generation, born Nov. 20, 1692, married Hannah Edgerton and settled at West Farms. His dwelling was located where the late Tommy Hyde resided. The name is not to be found upon the records of a later date than 1737.

Birchard, John, was born on the other side of the water in 1628, and emigrated to the New World with his father, Thomas Birchard, at the age of seven years. After residing successively at Hartford and Saybrook, he came to Norwich in 1660 as one of the original thirty-five Proprietors. He was much esteemed by his fellow townsmen and by the citizens generally, serving as Town Clerk, Justice of the Peace, Deputy to the General Court and, for a time, Clerk of the County Court. He married Christian Andrews, July 1st, 1653, by whom he had fourteen (14) children. He married for a second wife Jane, the widow of Samuel Hyde, the Proprietor, and became the guardian of her minor children. He resided for a time at West Farms upon the original Hyde domain where O. L. Johnson now lives. He subsequently removed to Lebanon where he died in 1702.

Birchard, James, son of the above, was born in Norwich, July 16th, 1665. He early became a resident in West Farms. His dwelling was on " Birchard's Playne " a short distance south of the Franklin Cemetery and upon the same side of the highway. Public worship was sometimes held at his house on the Sabbath, before the completion of the First Church. He seems to have been an estimable member of society. He married Elizabeth Beckwith, by whom he had ten children. His long and useful life was ended here, but none of his name or blood now reside within the limits of the town.

Crocker, Samuel, was a son of Thomas, of New London, where he was born in 1677. He early purchased twenty acres of land of Capt. Joseph Tracy, on Little Lebanon hill, now Crocker hill. His dwelling was located upon the slope of the hill, about midway from the base to the summit, upon the west side of the highway. He seems to have been an active and influential member of the settlement. In 1716 he served on an important committee, and his name often appeared upon the records of the society at later dates. In 1722 he served as a selectman. He had children, Samuel, John, Jabez and Hannah, but his descendants of the name have long since ceased to be residents of the place.

Downer, Joseph, Sen., settled at West Farms before 1700. His residence was upon the old road in the north part of the Society, which is now discontinued. For site of dwelling see accompanying map.

He had sons, Andrew, Richard and Joseph, who were active at the organization of the Society. They all married and probably all settled at West Farms, where their names are to be found as late as 1737.

Durkee, Dea. John, son of John, of Ipswich, Mass., was born Nov. 23d, 1689. He at first settled at Gloucester in his native state, but about 1720 removed to West Farms. He purchased lands of John Waterman, Jr., upon Portipaug hill, and his dwelling was located a short distance south of where Charles T. Hazen now lives, and upon the same side of the highway. His wife, Mary, died in 1732. He married for a second wife in 1738, Hannah Adgate.

In 1735, he was elected to the office of deacon in the West Farms church. His descendants have not been numerous.

Elderkin, John, Carpenter and Millwright, we find successively at Boston, Dedham, New-London, and finally at Norwich, in 1664. He was termed one of the second class of Proprietors, and had two home lots granted to him.

John Elderkin, Jr., eldest son of the above, early became a settler upon the west bank of the Shetucket river near Lord's (then Elderkin's) Bridge, and his dwelling was located upon the precise spot that is now occupied by the large boarding house of the Messrs. A. & W. Sprague, in the village of Baltic. He was the proprietor of the saw and grain mills near by. He often acted officially in the new society, and was particularly designated to direct in the layout of suitable highways or roads from the outskirts of the settlement to the church. The name long since disappeared from our records.

Edgerton, Samuel, was the third son and fifth child of Richard, another of the Thirty-Five Proprietors of Norwich. He was born in May, 1670, and probably settled at West Farms before 1700. He erected his dwelling where James C. Griswold now lives. He was a petitioner for a separate ecclesiastical organization in 1716, and afterwards was frequently elected to fill important offices in the gift of the society. In 1703 he married Alice Ripley, of Windham. David, his sixth son, born Aug. 28, 1718, was the founder of the Edgerton School Fund. For his place of residence see accompanying map.

Edgerton, Joseph, was a younger brother of the above, being the fourth son of Richard. He also settled at West Farms shortly before 1700. His location was upon Lebanon Road and his dwelling was where the late Guilbert Lamb formerly resided. He was also a petitioner for a new ecclesiastical organization and was often entrusted with office. He married, in 1702, Experience Pratt, and had several children. He was the ancestor of Bela Edgerton, Esq., and of Hon. Alfred P. Edgerton, late member of Congress from Indiana.

Fillmore, Capt. John, son of John Fillmore, "Mariner," of Ipswich, Mass., was born March 18, 1702. At an early age he was apprenticed to a ship carpenter in Boston, where, constantly meeting with seafaring men, he soon imbibed a longing for their mode of life. After several years of pleading he at length wrung from his mother a reluctant consent, and shipped in the spring of 1723 for a fishing voyage upon the sloop "Dolphin," of Cape Ann.

The following August the "Dolphin" was surprised and captured off Newfoundland by the notorious pirate, Capt. John Phillips. One of the pirate's crew happening to be an old acquaintance of Fillmore, represented to the Captain that he would prove a valuable acquisition to the crew if he could be induced to join them. Accordingly, young Fillmore was taken off, but promised his liberty after two months of faithful service. At the expiration of the appointed time, he demanded his liberty, which was denied him for some frivolous reason. The Captain, however, promised upon his honor to liberate him at the end of three additional months. But at the expiration of these months, Phillips positively refused to release him, and Fillmore determined to effect his own escape at the earliest opportunity.

One night, about nine months after his capture, the pirates had a grand carousal and retired at a late hour. This seemed a favorable opportunity, and Fillmore determined to secure posession of the ship with the assistance of three fellow prisoners, one of whom, however, was overcome with fear at the decisive moment, so that but three individuals were left to cope with the entire crew. They knew that the pirates after their drinking would not rise till late in the morning, and made their arrangements to attack them when they should first come upon deck, making use of the carpenter's tools for weapons. About noon the Captain, Master, Boatswain and Quartermaster came upon deck. Soon the Master proceeded to take an observation, the Captain and Boatswain engaged in conversation and the Quartermaster returned to the cabin. Now was the moment. The three officers upon deck are felled by unexpected blows, and the Quartermaster rushing from the cabin meets a similar fate. The officers being thus disposed of it is a comparatively easy matter to compel the surrender of the crew who are still all below.

The vessel was taken direct to Boston by this little band of heroes, where they arrived May 3, 1724. The crew were convicted of piracy by a court of admiralty. This court presented Mr. Fillmore with a gun, silver hilted sword and curious tobacco box which belonged to Captain Phillips, and also with the silver shoe and knee buckles, and two gold rings which he used to wear. These trophies of a worthy ancestor are still preserved among his descendents.

Mr. Fillmore never returned to the sea. He married, Nov. 24, 1724, Mary Spiller, of Ipswich, and removed to Norwich West Farms. Here he continued to reside through a long life, strong in the confidence of his townsmen. He died Feb. 22, 1777.

Gager, John, the Proprietor, was the son of Dr. William Gager, who came to this country with Gov. Winthrop in 1630, and died the same year. John Gager, the original Proprietor as above, had sons John and Samuel, besides six daughters. John, the eldest son, died without issue.

Samuel removed to New Concord. John, the eldest son of Samuel, settled at West Farms, and his dwelling was where Henry L. M. Ladd now resides. He married Jerusha, a daughter of Job Barstow, and has had a good number of descendants who have been useful and reliable members of society.

Griswold, Samuel, son of Capt. Samuel, and grandson of Lieut. Francis Griswold, an original Proprietor of Norwich, was born about 1689. When a young man, he settled in the eastern section of West Farms in what is now the village of Baltic, and his dwelling was located where the Baltic House now stands. He was the ancestor of the late Caleb Griswold.

Hartshorne, Dea. David, was the sixth son of Thomas, of Reading, Mass., where he was born Oct. 18, 1657. He married, 1680, Rebecca, daughter of John Batchelor, and had four sons and one daughter. His latest residence in the Bay State was at Medfield. He purchased lands at West Farms in 1697, of Ensign Thomas Waterman, and removed thither soon afterwards. His place of residence was where Geo. E. Starkweather now lives. He was one of the original deacons of the church, selectman in 1709, and foremost in civil and ecclesiastical affairs till his death, in 1738. His descendants have been numerous and respectable. Of their number may be mentioned the brave Capt. Asa Hartshorne, who was slain at the battle of the Miamis, Aug. 20, 1794. See Note G.

Hartshorne, Jonathan, was an elder brother of the above, and they accompanied each other to the new settlement. His place of residence was upon the old Windham road where Horatio Hyde now lives. His name often appears upon the records of the society in connection with official trusts. The late Dr. Elijah Hartshorne was one of his descendants.

Hazen, Lieut. Thomas, emigrated from Boxford, Mass., to West Farms near the commencement of the last century, and settled upon the place which is now in the occupancy of E. P. Ladd, and which was held and improved by his descendants for several generations, and which has been but recently alienated. He was one of the Society Committee in 1716, and frequently held office thereafter. At this period, men of mature years and ripe experience had the preference for important official positions.

His wife Mary died in 1727, and he himself eight years later. He now has descendants in the place and vicinity.

Huntington, Christopher, one of the original Thirty-Five Proprietors of Norwich, was born in England about 1630, and emigrated to this country with his parents a few years later. He was a son of William and a grandson of Simon Huntington and Margaret Baret. He married, 1652, Ruth Rockwell of Windsor, and Christopher, his fourth child was born Nov. 1, 1660. This was the first male child born in Norwich.

Christopher, son of the first born male of Norwich and grandson of Christopher the Proprietor, settled at West Farms upon domain now in the occupancy of Azariah Huntington, his great-grandson. He was a pillar in the church and society in his day. Several of his descendants have held official positions in the church. Rev. Asahel, of Topsfield, Mass., the father of Judge Huntington of Salem was of his line of descent.

Hyde, Samuel, another of the Thirty-five Proprietors, was the only son of William, also a Proprietor, and was born at Hartford in 1636. He married, 1659, Jane, daughter of Thomas Lee, of East Saybrook, now Lyme, and in the month of August of the year following, had daughter Elizabeth, who was the first female child born in Norwich of English descent. Shortly afterward she removed to West Farms, where, probably, his six remaining children were all born. He settled in the valley east of Meeting House hill and his dwelling was upon the site where O. L. Johnson, one of his descendants, now lives. He died in 1677.

Hyde, John, second son of the above, born at West Farms 1667. Married Experience Abell and settled at Wawekus Hill. But his fourth son, Capt. Matthew Hyde married Elizabeth Huntington and returned to West Farms which became permanently his place of residence. For site of his dwelling see accompanying map.

His descendants have been numerous and respectable. The late Rev. Eli Hyde was of the number.

Hyde, Thomas, fourth son of Samuel, born at West Farms in July, 1672, married Mary Backus and remained upon the paternal homestead. He was familiarly called the First Thomas Hyde. His eldest son born in 1699 the Second, and Capt. Thomas, first born of the "second" Thomas, and father of the late Jared Hyde, the Third Thomas Hyde. He was a useful member of society and his descendants have been numerous and highly respectable. Of some of the more distinguished may be mentioned the names of Rev. Alvan Hyde, D. D., of Rev. John Hyde, of Rev. Lavius Hyde and of the Hon. E. H. Hyde, present Lieut. Gov. of the State.

Hyde, Capt. Jabez, the fifth and youngest son of Samuel, was born at West Farms, 1677. He married Elizabeth, youngest daughter of Captain Richard Bushnell, and had his dwelling at the foot of Crocker Hill upon Lebanon road, where Dwight Fargo now resides. He was the first Clerk of the society, and continued to hold the office for a long term of years. He was also a Justice of the Peace and represented the town of Norwich thirteen sessions in the Colonial Legislature. He was the owner of a large landed estate and was accounted a prosperous farmer. He died Sept 5, 1762. His descendants have been numerous and have filled an important place in society here and elsewhere. The late Judge John Hyde, and Lewis Hyde, Esq., both of Norwich, were of his line of descent.

Johnson, John, was at West Farms as early as 1677. His place was in " Lebanon Valley," and his dwelling upon the site now occupied by the mansion of Bela T. Hastings. William and Ebenezer were probably his sons, and Dea. Isaac Johnson was his grandson. His descendants, though not numerous, have filled no unimportant place in society.

Kingsbury, Dea. Joseph, came early from Haverhill, Mass., to West Farms, with wife Love (Ayer) and sons Joseph and Ephraim. He erected his dwelling upon Middle of Center Hill on domain that has never been alienated by his descendants of the name. He was chairman of the meeting at which the society was organized in 1716, and was chosen one of the first deacons of the church two years later. He died in 1741. His son, Capt. Joseph Kingsbury, succeeded him as an officer of the church in 1735, and also held other important trusts, being selectman in 1723, and a representative to the General Court five sessions, from 1731 to 1742. He married Ruth Dennison, who, at the time of her decease at the age of 93 years, left 231 descendants.

The descendants of Joseph Kingsbury, Sen., have been numerous and have done not a little to shape the history of the town. Andrew, of Hartford, for a long time State Treasurer, and the late Col. Jacob, of Franklin, and Judge John, of Waterbury, were of the number.

Ladd, David, was an early settler and resided upon Pleasure Hill on the same premises that were owned and occupied till very recently by his descendant, Joseph D. Ladd. He married Mary Waters and had sons, Samuel, Ezekiel and Joseph.

Ladd, Nathaniel, was also an early settler and resided upon the place lately occupied by Benjamin Blackman. He was an individual of con siderable prominence in civil and ecclesiastical affairs, having served as selectman in 1721 and having been chosen to important offices in the society. He married and had several children born here, but ceased to be a resident about 1728. This place was subsequently owned and improved by David Ladd, probably a brother of Nathaniel.

Lathrop, Israel, third son of Samuel, who emigrated to Norwich as one of the second class of Proprietors in 1668, and grandson of Rev. John, an Independent minister in London, and afterwards in Scituate and Barnstable, had seven sons who, according to tradition, settled upon seven hills.

William Lathrop, second son of Israel, settled on Plain Hill and had ten sons. The late Jesse Lathrop of this place was his grandson. John L. Motley, the Historian, descended from him through Rev. John Lathrop, D. D., of Boston.

Serj. Israel Lathrop, Jr., another son of Israel, came to West Farms early and settled upon Blue Hill. His dwelling was upon the eastern declivity of the hill. For its particular site see accompanying map.

Capt. John Lathrop, also son of Israel, Sen., settled early upon Meeting House Hill. His dwelling was near the present residence of Joseph A. Griffin. Clergymen and distinguished individuals from abroad were often his guests during their temporary sojourn in the place.

The names of Serj. Israel, Jr., and Capt. John Lathrop often appear upon the records of the Society, which would indicate that they rendered important services which were duly appreciated.

Those bearing the name of Lathrop in this vicinity at this day, descended from William and Israel, Jr.

Mason, Jeremiah, son of David and Dorothy (Hobert) Mason, grandson of Lieut. Daniel, and great-grandson of the famous Major John Mason, early settled at West Farms upon lands bordering upon Lebanon. This estate is still in the name, and his dwelling was upon the same site if it is not the same structure that is now occupied by his lineal descendant, James F. Mason. His name often appears upon the records and always in relations that would show him to be a leading man. He was the ancestor of the late Hon. Jeremiah Mason, United States Senator from New Hampshire.

Mosely, Increase, was an early settler at West Farms. He probably resided where the tenant house of John Frink now stands. He was one

of the petitioners for a society organization in 1716, and his name thereafter occasionally appears upon the early records. He died in 1731.
Had a son Increase, born in 1712, who married Deborah Tracy, of
Windham, and removed to Woodbury about 1740 where he became a
distinguished civilian. Also had a son Peabody, born in 1724, who
married Mary, the eldest daughter of Captain Jacob Hyde, and became
a Baptist clergyman. His field of labor was first at Norwich. He
afterwards preached at Mansfield and Granby in this State. About the
year 1780 he joined the society of Shakers at New Lebanon, New York.

Peck, Benjamin, was a descendant of Henry, of New Haven, and
came hither before 1700. His dwelling was where the house of H. H.
Willes now stands. The stated worship on the Sabbath was held at
Benjamin Peck's house in the winter and at his barn in the summer,
till the first church was ready for use.

In 1720 the Society "Voted Benjamin Peck 15 shillings for half an
acre of land on Birchard's Playne, where he buried his daughter Elizabeth, for a Burying Place." This early action of the Society resulted
in the permanent location of the Franklin Cemetery, which has been
twice enlarged since. The selection proved to be most judicious. He
died in 1742. His offspring has been somewhat numerous—the late
Capt. Bela Peck, of Norwich, being of the number.

Pember, John, was the son of Thomas and Agnes Pember, of New
London, where he was born in 1698. He married, 1716, Mary,
daughter of the First Thomas Hyde. He became the first sexton at
West Farms. This office was successively filled by his descendants for
several generations. His dwelling was where Col. G. Pendleton now
resides. He died in 1783. Although his descendants have not been
numerous, the name is still to be found in the town.

Pettis, Samuel, was an early settler on Blue Hill. His descendants
have successivaly improved the same estate till recently. The late
Peter Pettis, who inherited both the homestead and the peculiarities of
his ancestor, was the last to bear the name.

Reynolds, Joseph, son of Joseph and grandson of John, the Proprie-
tor, was an early settler at West Farms, and had his dwelling where
Joseph I. Hyde now resides. He married in 1717, Hannah Bingham.
In 1723 he served as a member of the Prudential Committee of the
Society but soon afterwards alienated his estate to Job Barstow, and the
name disappeared from the records.

Rood, Micah, the youngest son of Thomas Rood, who was an early settler upon the east side of the Shetucket, removed in 1699 to West Farms, and located in Peck Hollow. Micah had upon his farm an apple tree which bore large, fair fruit, but always with a red globule, like a clot of blood, near the center of each apple. The apple, which has become a great favorite in this vicinity, and is called the *Mike* apple, from its originator,* still retains this peculiarity and is the object of much curious inquiry. The drop of blood invariably found in every apple is a standing wonder in childhood's days, and the story of its origin handed down from father to son for over a hundred years, has at length grown to be a fixed tradition, implicitly received. As the story runs, a pedlar entered town, vending such costly and luxurious wares as had never before been seen in the settlement. The simple Micah, dazzled by the display, invited the pedlar to his house, and at an evil moment plunged a knife to his heart beneath this very tree, so that his life blood flowed down and mingled with its roots. The next spring its blossoms changed from snowy white to red, and in August when the apples came tumbling down, large and yellow and juicy, horror of horrors, there hung in every one a drop of blood. There they lay before the terrified Micah, the evidences of his now never to be forgotten deed. With nature in springtime and autumn so strangely prompting the goadings of his conscience, who shall wonder that the simple-hearted Micah should change into a morose and melancholy man, and lead an accursed life? Such was the fact. Time went for naught but the memory of his crime, business was neglected, and soon from a prosperous farmer he became a pauper, dependent upon the charities of the community. In 1717 he was glad to increase his slender means by assuming charge of the meeting house, receiving therefor a peck of corn yearly from each family in the society.†

Of his last years and pauper's death the records tell briefly but significantly :—

July 5, 1727. The inhabitants do now, by their vote, agree to allow to each man that watches with Micah Rood, two shillings per night. Also to those who have attended sd Rood by day, three shillings per day.

December 17, 1728. To Jacob Hyde for digging Micah Rood's grave, £0, 4s, od.

---

* Thirty years ago it was called indifferently the *Mike*, or the *Rood* apple, but now the former name has generally obtained.

† October ye first day, 1717. Ye society agreed by their vote yt each family shall give Micah Rood a Peck of Corn for sweeping ye Meeting House one year.

In face of the facts, who shall pronounce the story of Micah Rood a fiction, or think it too strange that Nature should thus record her horror of human crime?

Rudd, Serj. Nathaniel, was a son of Jonathan, of Saybrook. He early settled at West Farms, and his dwelling was on the Portipaug Road a short distance north of Smith's Corners. He was chairman of the first committee elected by the society after its organization, and besides, took a prominent part in the civil affairs of the settlement. By first marriage in 1685 to Mary Post, he had son Jonathan and three daughters. By second marriage in 1705–6 to Abigail Hartshorne, had son Nathaniel and other children. He died in 1727.

Rudd, Jonathan, eldest son of the above, was born at West Farms, May 22, 1693. He married, Oct. 27, 1720, Joanna Gregory of Stratford, and had five children. His name often occurs upon the records of the society in official relations. His almost life-long residence was in a rural situation on the hill in a north-westerly direction from that of his father. He died in 1772. Five years afterwards his late dwelling was used as a pest house where soldiers from the army were inoculated and treated for small pox. It was then that his son Jonathan, at the time the occupant of the premises, fell a victim to that disease.

It was in this secluded retreat, with wild surroundings, that the young and talented Ebenezer Hartshorne first met the amiable and accomplished Miss Miriam Gregory, of Stratford, whom he afterwards wedded and with whom he lived for a period of sixty-five years in the enjoyment of domestic bliss unalloyed. Their early and romantic correspondence is still extant.

Rudd, Nathaniel, Jun., son of Serj. Nathaniel, had his dwelling where John Q. Cross now lives. He married, Dec. 22, 1730, Mary Backus, and had a numerous family of children.

Sabin, Capt. John, was born in Pomfret, Conn., 1696. He came to West Farms soon after the organization of the society, and had his residence where John Frink now lives. He acted a prominent part in civil and ecclesiastical affairs in his time. His death occurred March 28, 1742. He was a maternal ancestor of Hon. L. F. S. Foster. See Physicians, Note G.

Sluman, Thomas, son of Thomas and Sarah (Bliss) Sluman, was an early settler at West Farms, and had his residence and place of busines near the Peck Hollow station on the New London and Northern Rail

Road, where he had a saw and corn mill for this part of the settlement. His name is on the petition for the organization of a new society in 1716, and two years later he acted upon a committee which petitioned the General Assembly for the organization of a church. Although he took an active part in ecclesiastical affairs in his day, the name has long since ceased to be found upon the records.

Smith, Serj. Obadiah, afterwards called Captain, was a son of Edward, and a grand-nephew of Nehemiah Smith, the Proprietor. He married a daughter of Joshua Abell, and early settled at West Farms. His dwelling was where Edward A. Allyn now resides. He was one of the petitioners for the organization of a new society, and a member of the first committee of the society after its organization. He was active and useful in the settlement to the time of his death in 1727, at the age of 50 years. His descendants, though not numerous, have ever been found in the place. He was the ancestor of the late Rev. Joshua Smith, and of A. B. Smith, now Postmaster of Franklin.

Tracy, Lieut. Thomas, the Proprietor, came from Tewksbury in Gloucestershire, to New England in 1636. After residing for a short time at Salem, Mass., he removed to Wethersfield, Conn., and a few years later to Saybrook. When a resident at this place in 1645, he, with others, relieved Uncas, the Sachem of Mohegan, with provisions when he was besieged at Shattuck's Point by Pessechus, Sachem of the Narragansets; which led to the subsequent grant of the town of Norwich in 1659. In 1660 he came to Norwich as one of the pioneer settlers. He was evidently a leading man in this new locality, for in addition to other important appointments which he received, his name is on the roll of the Legislature as a representative from Norwich at twenty-seven sessions.

By his first marriage to the widow of Edward Mason, at Wethersfield, he had six sons and a daughter. He died Nov. 7, 1685, at the age of 75 years.

Tracy, Capt. John, eldest son of the above, born about 1643, was also classed as one of the Thirty-five Proprietors of Norwich. He settled very early at West Farms and had his dwelling where the late Almond Tracy resided. He was a Justice of the Peace, and represented the town of Norwich six sessions in the Colonial legislature. He married, June 10, 1670, Mary Winslow, a niece of Gov. Edward Winslow of Plymouth, and had sons John, Joseph and Winslow. He died in 1702, leaving an estate of between three and four thousand acres of land.

Tracy, John, 2d, eldest son of the above, born 1673, married Elizabeth Leffingwell, and settled upon the paternal homestead where his descendants continue to reside to the present time. He was the ancestor of Hon. Uri Tracy, a member of Congress from the State of New York, and of Hon. John Tracy, for six years Lieut. Gov. of the same state. Governor Tracy was the sixth John Tracy, each of his predecessors of the name representing a generation. These six John Tracys were in the line of primogeniture, and all natives of West Farms, except the first, who was the Proprietor.

Tracy, Capt. Joseph, second son of John, the Proprietor, was born at West Farms, April 20, 1682, and had his dwelling near the residence of the late J. W. Kingsley. He was a Justice of the Peace and representative of the town several sessions in the Colonial legislature. He married, Dec. 31, 1705, Mary, daughter of Caleb Abell, and had ten children. His second son, Dr. Elisha Tracy, graduated at Yale college in 1738, became a distinguished physician and settled near the Town Plot; was the father of the late Dr. Philemon Tracy and the ancestor of the Honorables Phineas Lyman Tracy and Albert Haller Tracy, both of whom were members of Congress from the State of New York.

Tracy, Serj. Winslow, third son of John, the Proprietor, was born at West Farms, Feb. 9, 1689. He married Rachel Ripley, and had his dwelling upon Windham road a short distance north of the Kingsbury mansion. He was a petitioner for a new ecclesiastical organization, and was for a long time an active and influential member of society. Col. Uriah Tracy, member of Congress and United States Senator from Connecticut, was his grandson.

Waterman, Thomas, the Proprietor, was the second son of Robert, of Marshfield, where he was born, 1644. He married Miriam, daughter of Lieut. Thomas Tracy, and had sons Thomas and John. Thomas, the eldest, married, June 20, 1691, Elizabeth Allyn, and had seven sons and two daughters. Ensign Thomas Waterman, the eldest, settled at West Farms, and had his residence on the old Waterman road northwest of the church. His name often appears upon the early records, and his homestead was successively occupied by several generations of his descendants, but none of his name or blood remain in the place.

Other individuals early appeared in the settlement whom we have not been able definitely to locate. Of these we would particularly mention William Moore, Jonathan Crain and Peter Cross. These persons were at most but temporary residents. The last two probably removed to that part of Windham which is now Mansfield.

Thomas Wood, the carpenter, Jonathan Roise (Royce), John Harris, Ebenezer Case and John Hutchens appeared at a later day. These individuals, also, after a residence of a few years, removed to other localities.

NOTE E.

COLLEGE GRADUATES.

This list is designed to include the names of those graduates of the different colleges of the country who have been raised up in Franklin, and who are generally natives of the place. When not to the manor born, their immediate and generally more remote ancestors have been so identified with the history of the town as to make it proper that their names should find a place in our catalogue.

YALE COLLEGE.

1738—Doctor Elisha Tracy,
1763—Sanford Kingsbury,
1767—Jonathan Kingsbury,
1769—Reverend David Avery,
1769—Reverend Charles Backus, D. D.,
1777—John Barker, M. D.,
1778—Honorable Uriah Tracy,
1786—Reverend Jonathan Ellis,
1786—Honorable John Kingsbury,
1787—Reverend Azel Backus, D. D.,
1788—Honorable Jeremiah Mason, LL. D.,
1789—Honorable Uri Tracy,
1803—Reverend Eli Hyde,
1803—Reverend John Hyde,
1806—Doctor John Hazen,
1815—Reverend Elijah Hartshorne,
1817—David Nevins Lord,
1819—Honorable Asahel Huntington,
1833—Reverend Joshua Smith,
1843—Reverend Robert Palmer Stanton,
1846—Reverend Joseph Willes Backus,
1850—Reverend George Sherman Converse,
1855—P. Henry Woodward,
1867—Richard William Woodward.

DARTMOUTH COLLEGE.

1785—Reverend Alvan Hyde, D. D.,
1786—Reverend Asahel Huntington,
1788—Reverend Oliver Ayer,
1794—Reverend Jabez Munsell,
1815—Elisha Huntington, M. D.

MIDDLEBURY COLLEGE.

1809—Bela Edgerton.

WILLIAMS COLLEGE.

1813—Reverend Lavius Hyde.

BROWN UNIVERSITY.

1795—Reverend Eliphalet Nott, D. D., LL.D.,
1828—Honorable LaFayette S. Foster, LL.D.

AMHERST COLLEGE.

1824—Reverend Beaufort Ladd.

UNION COLLEGE.

1808—Reverend Samuel Nott, Jr.,
1809—Reverend David Huntington,
1822—Reverend Stephen Tertius Nott,
1831—Orsamus H. Marshall, A. M.,
1834—Reverend Albert T. Chester, D. D.,
1846—Reverend John W. Nott,
1849—Anson Gleason Chester, A. M.

NOTE F.

A list of the Clergymen who have been raised up in Franklin, with brief sketches of some that have deceased.

Avery, Rev. David, son of John and Lydia (Smith) Avery, was born at West Farms, April 5, 1746. He became hopefully pious at an early age under the preaching of Whitfield, and shortly afterwards entered Moor's Indian Charity School in Lebanon with special reference to a collegiate education. By close application while here he was enabled to enter college a year in advance, and graduated at Yale in

1769. While in college he improved his vacations in instructing Indian youth in various localities. His theological education was under the direction of Rev. Eleazer Wheelock, D. D., of Dartmouth College. This having been completed, he was ordained as a missionary to the Oneida Indians, Aug. 29, 1771. As the result of an accident he was compelled to abandon this field of labor and return to New England. Two years later, March 25, 1773, he was installed at Gaysboro', (now Windsor, Vt.,), and from April 18, 1776 to Feb. 1, 1780, he served as a chaplain in the army.

After leaving the army he lived and preached at Wrentham, Mass., and various other places, till in 1817 he was invited to settle at Middletown, Va. On the evening of a day of fasting, preparatory to his installation, he was seized with typhus fever which soon carried him off. He married, Oct. 10, 1782, Hannah Chaplain of Mansfield, (now Chaplain), who with several children survived him.

Mr. Avery is said to have been tall, portly and commanding in appearance, with a prominent Roman countenance. In his disposition he was generous and warm hearted, being emphatically a gentleman of the old school. He preached extemporaneously, using at most but short notes. His language was copious and diffuse, his voice clear and sonorous, and his articulation so distinct that it was a common saying in the army that every soldier in the brigade could hear all that he said.

Ayer, Rev. Oliver, son of Joseph, Jr., and Mary (Bailey) Ayer, was born at West Farms, Nov. 14, 1765. He fitted for college under the instruction of Rev. Samuel Nott, his pastor, and graduated at Dartmouth in 1788. Having completed his theological course also with Rev. Samuel Nott, he was ordained at West Stockbridge, Mass., May 29, 1793. Here he remained, greatly beloved by his people till June 14, 1807, when he was dismissed. He was subsequently settled at Augusta, Richland and Sandy Creek, all in the State of New York, and was everywhere held in esteem for his ministerial fidelity. He died at Richland in July, 1832, at the ripe age of 67 years. While at West Stockbridge he married Phebe, a daughter of Elijah Brown of that place, who survived him.

Backus, Rev. Azel, D. D., of the sixth generation from William Backus, Sen., the Proprietor, was born at West Farms, October 13, 1765. He was the son of Jabez, Jr., and Deborah (Fanning) Backus, both of whom are said to have been persons of great excellence of character. His father dying when he was only five years of age, bequeathed to him a farm, which he says, "I wisely exchanged for an education in college." He graduated at Yale in the class of 1787.

While in college he had sceptical tendencies ; but his uncle, Rev. Charles Backus, D. D., by his faithful efforts won him from infidelity and reared him up for the ministry. He was ordained April 6th, 1791, as the immediate successor of Dr. Bellamy, at Bethlehem, where he not only labored faithfully as a pastor, but also instituted and conducted a school of considerable celebrity, at which a large number of young men were prepared for admission to college.

In Sept., 1812, Dr. Backus was elected first President of Hamilton College. His mature experience in the instruction and management of young men was doubtless greatly auxiliary to his success in this somewhat similar, though more extensive field of labor.

He was a man of an original cast of thought, distinguished by susceptibility and ardor of feeling ; was possessed, withal, of brilliant talents and rose rapidly in popular favor, for while comparatively a young man he was selected by the senior Gov. Oliver Wolcott to preach the annual election sermon before the Legislature of Conn. This appointment was fulfilled with very marked ability in 1798. In June, 1808, he was chosen moderator of the General Association of Conn., and two years later he was honored with the degree of Doctor of Divinity from the college in New Jersey.

Duyckinck remarks, that " His biography remains to be written in a manner worthy of the part which he sustained in caring for the first wants of a college," etc., and adds, that " A careful memoir written somewhat after the manner of Xenophon's Memorabilia, or Boswell's Johnson, would be welcomed by many readers."

Dr. Backus died Dec. 9, 1817, of typhus fever, which then prevailed in the college and vicinity. He married, in 1791, Melicent Demming, of Wethersfield, who with five children survived him. His daughter, Mary Ann, became the first wife of Hon. Gerret Smith, of Peterboro.

For a list of his publications reference may be had to Dr. Sprague's Annals of the Pulpit, Vol. II, page 283.

Backus, Rev. Charles, D. D., of the fifth generation from William Backus, Sen., the Proprietor, was born at West Farms, Nov. 4, 1749. He was the third son of Jabez, Sen., and Eunice (Kingsbury) Backus, both of whom he lost in childhood, but through the assistance of friends he was enabled to obtain a thorough classical education, and graduated at Yale in 1769. While in college he had a high reputation both for scholarship and deportment. Pres't Dwight, his classmate, said of him, " I have not known a wiser man." His theological education was under the direction of Levi Hart, D. D., of Preston. In 1775 he was ordained to the pastoral charge of the congregational church in Somers, Conn., in which place he remained till his death, Dec. 30, 1803. The sermon at his ordination was preached by Rev. John Ellis, of West Farms.

His high reputation as a theologian procured for him invitations from Yale and Dartmouth Colleges to occupy the chair of Theology in each of these institutions. These in each instance he modestly declined. But his eminence as an instructor drew around him many who were designed for the ministry. Nearly fifty young men were at different times members of his theological school. Among them were Dr. Woods, of Andover, Dr. Hyde, of Lee, Dr. Cooley of Granville, Pres't Moore, of Amherst College and many others of nearly equal distinction. In 1801 he received the honorary degree of D. D., from Williams College. Shortly after his settlement at Somers he was married to Bethia, daughter of Jacob Hill, of Cambridge, Mass. Jabez, their only child, died suddenly while a member of Yale College, March 16, 1794, in his seventeenth year.

The publications of Dr. Backus were numerous. From 1785 to 1798, he published twelve distinct sermons, besides five discourses on the divine authority of the scriptures, in 1797. For a more particular description reference may be had to Dr. Sprague's Annals, Vol. II, p. 62.

Backus, Rev. Joseph W., is now pastor of the Congregational Church at Thomaston, Conn.

Chester, Rev. Albert T., D. D., is a Presbyterian clergyman; resides in Buffalo, N. Y., and is Principal of a flourishing female academy located in that city.

Converse, Rev. George S., is an Episcopal clergyman and at the present time is Rector of St. James' church, at Roxbury, Mass.

Ellis, Rev. Jonathan, sixth son of Rev. John Ellis, was born at West Farms, April 11, 1762. He fitted for college under the instruction of his father and graduated at Yale in the class of 1786. Devoting the requisite period to a theological course of reading, he was ordained pastor of the congregational church at Topsham, Maine, in 1789. This connection continued till 1810, when he was dismissed, and on the following year deposed from the ministry on account of charges against his moral character. He was actively interested in the establishment of Bowdoin College and a candidate for the Professorship of Languages, and would probably have succeeded in securing the situation except for the " Harvard " influence which was brought to bear upon

La Fayette S. Foster

the appointment. He was a good linguist and quite a number of scholars were prepared for admission to college under his instruction. It is said that he was also something of a poet. He published a eulogy in verse on Washington, delivered Feb. 22, 1800.

After residing a few years at Bath, he left his eastern home unaccompanied by any member of his family, and never returned. Previous to 1827, letters were occasionally received from him, but later his family had no trace of his whereabouts. For a time he was engaged in teaching in Pennsylvania, but when last heard from was in Delaware. He married, in 1790, Mary Fulton, of Topsham, by whom he had ten children. She lived to an advanced age. One son, Asher Ellis, received the degree of M. D., at Bowdoin College in 1832, and settled at Brunswick, Maine. Another son, Rev. Robert Fulton Ellis, became a Baptist clergyman.

Ellis, Rev. Stephen, son of Stephen and Rebecca (Huntington) Ellis, was born at Franklin, April 16, 1801. At an early age his parents removed to Pennsylvania. Shortly afterwards he left his home and entered the school of a maternal cousin, Rev. John C. Rudd, D. D., at Elizabethtown, New Jersey, where he remained as pupil and assistant teacher for about ten years. Having thus acquired a tolerably thorough preliminary education, he entered upon the study of theology under the direction of a Presbyterian clergyman in Elizabethtown, where by close application he made rapid progress. In 1830 he was licensed by the New London Association at New London, and soon thereafter preached his first sermon at Franklin. After preaching three years at West Stafford, Conn., where he declined an invitation to settle permanently in the ministry, and two or three years in Susquehanna county, Pennsylvania, he was finally ordained at Great Bend, Pa., in 1836. After several years of faithful service at this place, he removed to Delaware county, New York, first to the town of Meredith, and finally to the village of Davenport, where he died Aug. 13, 1848, of dysentery. He was everywhere esteemed as a faithful pastor. He also labored actively and heartily to advance the benevolent enterprises of the age, even to the end of life. In 1831, he married Lydia A. Mott, a resident of his native place, who with one daughter survives him.

Fillmore, Rev. Amaziah, eldest son of Comfort and Zerviah (Bosworth) Fillmore, and grandson of the famous Capt. John Fillmore, was born at West Farms, Sept. 26, 1765, and early became a local preacher of the Methodist Episcopal church. He was licensed as an exhorter,

March 2, 1799, at Norwich, by Shadrich Bostwick, Presiding Elder,
ordained Deacon June 6, 1810, by Bishop Asbury, and ordained an
Elder June 13, 1823, at Providence, by Bishop George. He preached
many years before he was ordained Deacon or Elder, but his labors
were then and afterwards confined to his native town and the immediate
vicinity. He died April 5, 1847.

Fillmore, Rev. Comfort Day, youngest brother of the above, was
born at Franklin, July 8, 1792, and also became a local Methodist
preacher. He took ministerial license about 1828, and Deacon's orders
in 1834, from Bishop Hedding. He also received from the same
prelate, Elder's orders in 1845. His field of labor was in his native
town and vicinity. His services were particularly sought for upon
funeral occasions. In 1848 he removed to the adjoining town of Lisbon, and again in 1859, to Norwich, where he died July 9, 1867.

Fillmore, Rev. Daniel, eldest son of Rev. Amaziah Fillmore, was
born at Franklin, Dec. 29, 1787. Having well improved such advantages as the common district schools of Connecticut then afforded for
an education, he joined the Methodist Itinerancy in June, 1811, and
was appointed to the Falmouth circuit in Maine. He early rose to an
honorable position among his brethren, and filled many of the most
important stations in New England, as at Portland, Me., Portsmouth,
N. H., Boston, Charlestown, Lynn, Nantucket and New Bedford,
Mass., and Providence, R. I. To each of these stations he was re-ap-
pointed and remained two years at each term. He was for many years
Secretary of the New England Conference, the duties of which office
he discharged with distinguished ability. He was also an ardent and
active friend of education in the church, and for several years performed
the duties of financial agent of the Wesleyan University for the Providence Conference.

As one of the founders of Methodism, he most cheerfully shared in
the labors, struggles and poverty of its early years, and lived to witness
its successes and triumphs ; and to but few men in New England is this
branch of the church more indebted for its present prosperity. In
1852 he was put upon the superannuated list. It may be said of him,
that he was one of the first generation of Methodist preachers in New
England, most of whom have passed away. He died at Providence,
R. I., Aug. 13, 1858, leaving an example of christian faithfulness and
ministerial fidelity worthy of imitation.

Fillmore Rev. Hiel, fourth son of Rev. Amaziah Fillmore, was born
at Franklin, July 27, 1795, and became a local preacher of the Metho-

dist Episcopal Church, as did his father before him. In 1823 he was authorized to exhort and hold meetings, by Isaac Jennison, a circuit preacher. In 1832 he was ordained a Deacon at Providence, by Bishop Hedding, and in 1846 was ordained an Elder at Norwich Falls, by Bishop Waugh. He preached and performed other ministerial labors in his own town and neighborhood as his services were required. He died at Norwich, whither he had removed a few years previous, July 27, 1862.

Fillmore, Rev. Jesse, is a Methodist clergyman, who now resides at Providence, Rhode Island.

Hartshorne, Rev. Elijah, Jr., son of Doctor Elijah Hartshorne, was born at Franklin in 1790. Under the instruction of his pastor, Rev. Samuel Nott, he was prepared for college and graduated at Yale in the class of 1815. A few years later he was licensed as a preacher, and temporarily supplied many pulpits in the vicinity, but was never ordained. He died at Franklin, Sept. 19, 1840, unmarried.

Huntington, Rev. Asahel, son of Barnabas and Anne (Wright) Huntington, of the sixth generation from Simon Huntington, the emigrant ancestor of the family, was born at West Farms, March 17, 1761. He was prepared for college under the teaching of his pastor, Rev. Samuel Nott, and entered Dartmouth where he graduated in 1786 with the first honors of his class. His theological studies were pursued under instruction of the Rev. Doctors Backus, of Somers, and Hart, of Griswold. He was ordained and settled as pastor of the congregational church at Topsfield, Mass., Nov. 12, 1789. After a faithful ministry of nearly twenty-four years to a devoted people, he died suddenly at this place, April 22, 1813, of malignant sore throat. He married, June 2, 1791, Alethea, daughter of Doctor Elisha Lord, of Pomfret, Conn. The late Doctor Elisha Huntington, of Lowell, and the Hon. Asahel Huntington, of Salem, were his sons.

Huntington, Rev. David, son of Ezra and Elizabeth (Huntington) Huntington, of the sixth generation from Simon Huntington, the immigrant ancestor of the family, was born at Franklin, April 24, 1788. He was prepared for college under the instruction of Rev. Samuel Nott, and entered Union at Schenectady, where he graduated in 1809. He studied theology, and was ordained Deacon of the Protestant Episcopal Church, by Bishop Hobart, in Trinity church, New York City in 1812; and was ordained Priest in St. Paul's church, at Charlton, N. Y., three years later. He was a devoted Episcopalian, though it is said that he did not class himself either with the High Church or Low Church party, maintaining that those who went beyond, or fell below the accepted standards of the church, were equally in error. For several of his last years he resided at Harpersville, N. Y., without parochial charge. He died at this place, April 9, 1855.

Hyde, Rev. Alvan, D. D., son of Joseph Hyde by his first wife, Abigail Abell, being of the sixth generation from William Hyde, the Proprietor, was born at West Farms, Feb. 2, 1768. He was prepared for college by his pastor, Rev. Samuel Nott, and graduated at Dartmouth in the class of 1788. In the autumn of 1789, he placed himself under the instruction of the Rev. (afterwards Dr.) Charles Backus, of Somers, as a theological teacher, and was licensed to preach by the Tolland Association of Congregational ministers the year following. At the earnest solicitation of the church and society in Lee, Mass., he was ordained to the work of the gospel ministry in that place, June 6, 1792. The sermon on the occasion was preached by Rev. (afterwards Dr.) Samuel Nott.

It is said that Dr. Hyde's manner in the pulpit was solemn, grave and earnest, but never impassioned. He spoke as one who felt that "he must give account," and whose only aim was to win souls to Christ by a clear and simple presentation of gospel truth. He had a high reputation as a theological teacher, and assisted, at different times, between thirty and forty young men in their preparation for the ministry. He was also an active friend and patron of Williams College, and was in some way officially connected with that institution for more than thirty years. He died at his post, at Lee, Dec. 4, 1833, after an eminently successful ministry of more than forty-one years' continuance. An interesting memoir of him was published in 1835. In April, 1703, he was married to Lucy, daughter of Benjamin Fessenden of Sandwich, Mass. Of their eleven children only six survived the father.

Of his publications a list may be found in Dr. Sprague's Annals, Vol. II, page 303.

Hyde, Rev. Charles, is a Congregational clergyman who has retired from the pastoral office and now resides at Ellington, Conn.

Hyde, Rev. Eli, third son of Eli and Rhoda (Lathrop) Hyde, and great-grandson of John Hyde of the third generation, was born at West Farms, Jan. 20th, 1778. He was prepared for college by his pastor, Rev. Samuel Nott, and graduated at Yale in the class of 1803.

After a thorough theological course of reading under the instruction of Rev. Doctors Calvin Chapin, of Wethersfield, and Ciprian Strong, of Chatham, he was ordained as a Presbyterian clergyman, at Oxford, N. Y., in the spring of 1808. After a ministry of about four years at this place, he was dismissed, and afterwards, in the summer of 1812, he devoted several months to missionary labor in northern New York, then but sparsely settled. The next year he was installed in the ministry at Amenia in the same State, and subsequently at Salem, Conn., and Salisbury, Vt. As a religious teacher, he was eminently sound and scriptural in his theological views, and as a pastor, faithful and devoted to his consecrated work. He died at Franklin, Oct. 3, 1856. In Nov. 1807, he was married to Sarah, daughter of Rev. Samuel Nott, who still survives him.

Hyde, Rev. John, eldest son of Vaniah and Rebecca (Barker) Hyde, and great-grandson of Thomas Hyde of the third generation from William, the Proprietor, was born at West Farms, July 7, 1776. Having been prepared for college by his pastor, Rev. Samuel Nott, he entered Yale, where he graduated in the class of 1803. After devoting the usual period to a theological course under Rev. Asahel Hooker, then of Goshen, but afterwards of Norwich, Conn., he was ordained pastor of the Congregational church at Hamden, Conn., in April, 1806, which charge he resigned after a ministry of about five years. He was installed in 1812 pastor of the church in Preston, Conn., where he remained fifteen years. He was then dismissed, and in the spring of 1828 was again installed at North Wilbraham, Mass., where he remained about five years. After this he preached in various places, but did not again become a settled pastor. Mr. Hyde died at Franklin, much respected and beloved, Aug. 14, 1848, aged 72 years. He married, April 22, 1806, Susan, daughter of Rev. Samuel Nott. She died at West Killingly in 1842.

Hyde, Rev. Larius, third son of Joseph Hyde by his second wife, Julitta Abell, and great-grandson of Thomas of the third generation, being the sixth from William Hyde, the Proprietor, was born at Franklin, Jan. 29, 1789. He graduated at Williams College in 1813, studied theology at Andover, and was ordained pastor of the Congregational church at Salisbury, Conn., in 1818. In 1824 he was installed over the church in Bolton, Conn., and was afterwards pastor at Ellington, Conn., Wayland and Becket, Mass., and was finally re-settled at Bolton. When 70 years of age, in accordance with a previously expressed purpose, he retired from the pastoral office and became a resident at Vernon. Mr. Hyde was a man of extensive research and of rare attainments.

He was the author of an interesting memoir of his half-brother, Rev. Alvan Hyde, D. D., published in 1835, and was the friend and literary executor of Carlos Wilcox, and published his biography, with selections from his writings. He was possessed of much warmth of religious feeling, and was everywhere regarded as a faithful and devoted pastor. He died at Vernon, April 3, 1865. He was married in 1818, to Alice Bradley, of Stockbridge, Mass., who, with one son and three daughters, survives him.

Ladd, Rev. Beaufort, is a retired Congregational clergyman who, at the present time, resides at Victory, Cayuga county, N. Y.

Moseley, Rev. Peabody, son of Increase and Mary Moseley, born at West Farms, Aug. 19, 1724, became a Baptist clergyman and resided and preached successively at Norwich, Mansfield, and Granby, Conn. He married Mary, eldest daughter of Capt. Jacob Hyde, Aug. 2, 1748. About the year 1780, he and his wife and a part of his children, joined the society of Shakers at New Lebanon, N. Y., where he died in Sept., 1791. Mrs. Moseley survived him about 25 years, and finally died with the Shakers at New Lebanon.

Munsell, Rev. Jabez, youngest son of Henry and Sarah (Hyde) Munsell, was born at West Farms, about 1769. He was prepared for college under Rev. Samuel Nott, and graduated at Dartmouth in the class of 1794; took a second degree at Yale in 1799; was settled as a Congregational minister at Gill, Mass., in 1802; resigned his charge in 1805, and removed to Richmond, Va., where he died in 1832.

Nott, Rev. Eliphalet, D. D., son of Stephen and Deborah (Selden) Nott, being of the fifth generation from John Nott, Sen., of Wethersfield, was born at Ashford, Conn., June 25, 1773, but Franklin early became his adopted home. It is said that he was favored with an excellent mother; and it is, doubtless, due to the fostering care of this tireless woman, that the foundations for his future eminence were early and securely laid. His subsequent preliminary education was acquired mainly under the instruction of his brother, Rev. Samuel Nott, D. D. Although he received the degree of Master of Arts from Brown University in 1795, he had not the benefit of a regular collegiate course of instruction; but the want of this, however, was compensated by a natural facility in acquiring knowledge. Having studied theology under the Rev. Joel Benedict, D. D., of Plainfield, Conn., he was licensed and sent out as a *Missionary* to Central New York. Not long afterwards, he established himself as a clergyman and principal of an academy at Cherry Valley, then a frontier settlement in that state. In

1798 he become pastor of the Presbyterian church, in Albany, where he remained for the next six years, and at this period he had few equals in pulpit eloquence in the country. In 1804 he delivered his very eloquent discourse upon the death of Hamilton which, doubtless, secured his appointment in that year, as fourth President of Union College. He continued to manage the affairs of this Institution with extraordinary ability for a period of more than sixty years, and under his guidance such men as Francis Wayland, William H. Seward and Judge Kent, were raised up to shed luster upon the present age.

President Nott, in his intercourse with his pupils, had the rare faculty of inspiring in them a sense of self-respect, and o calling forth their earnest, manly qualities of head and heart. Of an original cast of mind, developed by elaborate culture, he had large inventive powers, which he did not fail to devote to useful purposes, for he took out, at different times, more than thirty patents for the generation and application of heat, including that for the celebrated stove bearing his name.

He died at Schenectady, Jan. 29, 1866, aged 92 years.

His published works are, Addresses to Young Men, Temperance Addresses, and a volume of Sermons.

Nott, Rev. John W., is an Episcopal clergyman; resides at Frostburgh, Md., and is without parochial charge. He is at present employed in teaching.

Nott, Rev. Samuel, Jr., son of Rev. Samuel Nott, D. D., and Lucretia (Taylor) Nott, was born in Franklin, Sept. 11, 1788. He was prepared for college by his father, and entered Union, where he graduated in 1808. He then entered the theological seminary at Andover, where he remained about one year. Having obtained a ministerial license, he preached in various pulpits during the next two or three years, after which he was ordained in the Tabernacle church, at Salem, Mass., Feb. 6, 1812, with Newell, Judson, Hall and Rice, and the same month sailed for Calcutta to enter the foreign field as a missionary to the heathen, being one of the little band of pioneers sent forth by the American Board of Commissioners for Foreign Missions, then but recently organized. He returned from India to this country in Aug., 1816. Shortly afterwards he took charge of a school composed of young ladies, in the city of New York, which he continued to conduct till the spring of 1823, when he removed to Galway, in the same state, and became the pastor of the Presbyterian church in that place. This relation was dissolved in 1829, when he removed to Wareham, Mass., and became the pastor of the Congregational church in that town. He was dismissed from this charge in 1846, but continued to reside in the place for the next twenty years, employed much of the time in teaching. The last year of his life was passed at the residence of his son, in Hartford, Conn., where he died June 1, 1869. He married, Feb. 8, 1812, Roxanna Peck, also of Franklin, who with their seven children survives him.

His published works, most of which appeared at an early date, are "Sermons for Children," 3 vols.; "Sermons from the Fowls of the Air and Lilies of the Field"; "Sermons on Public Worship"; "Appeal to the Temperate"; "Temperance and Religion"; "Freedom of the Mind"; "The Telescope"; "A Sermon on the Idolatry of the Hindoos"; "A Discourse on the Death of President Harrison"; etc.

Nott, Rev. Stephen T., youngest son of Rev. Samuel Nott, D. D., was born at Franklin, June 20, 1802. He fitted for college under the instruction of his father, and graduated at Union in 1822. He also acquired a competent knowledge of theology under the paternal roof; obtained a ministerial license from the New London Association of Congregational ministers, and preached in a number of pulpits in this and the adjoining States, but was never ordained. He died at the family mansion in Franklin, July 23, 1828, unmarried.

Prentice, Rev. Erastus L., is a Methodist clergyman; belongs to the New York Conference, and resides at Poughkeepsie in that State.

Rudd, Rev. John Churchill, D. D., son of Jonathan and Mary (Huntington) Rudd, was born at West Farms, May 24, 1779. He was prepared for Yale College by Rev. Samuel Nott, but from adverse circumstances he was prevented from taking a collegiate course. He was educated a congregationalist, but it is said that he felt some difficulty, even at an early period, respecting the distinctive features of Calvinism, and the result of his reading and reflection was only to establish him in the Episcopal system; and he was accordingly admitted to Deacon's Orders, by Bishop Moore in 1805, and to Priests' Orders by the same venerable prelate the year following. After a few months of missionary labor on Long Island, at the suggestion of Bishop Moore, he took charge of St. John's Parish, Elizabethtown, N. J., and shortly afterwards was instituted its rector. While at this place, he edited the "Churchman's Magazine," a religious periodical. In 1826 he resigned his charge in consequence of failing health and voice, and removed to Auburn, N. Y., to take charge of an academy. The year following he commenced another religious periodical, "The Gospel Messenger," which he continued to conduct to the end of his life. In 1822 he received the honorary degree of D. D., from the University of Pennsylvania. Dr. Rudd died at Utica, N. Y., Nov. 15, 1848. He married, in 1803, Phebe Eliza, daughter of Edward Bennet, of Shrewsbury, N. J., but had no children.

Smith, Rev. Joshua, second son of Joshua and Elizabeth (Hartshorne) Smith, was born at Franklin, March 1, 1809. After a thorough preparation for college, he graduated at Yale in the class of 1833. He was subsequently employed for some time in teaching, and then entered the theological seminary at Alexandria, Va., to qualify himself for the ministry of the Protestant Episcopal Church. After graduating at the seminary, he was ordained Deacon by the Rt. Rev. Richard Channing Moore, Jan. 10, 1840, and shortly after went as a missionary of the Protestant Domestic and Foreign Missionary Society, to Cape Palmas, Western Africa. He returned to the United States in 1844, and resided successively at Batavia, Rochester and Buffalo, N. Y., and finally removed to Newark, N. J., in 1853. He was ordained Priest by Bishop Doane, April 28, 1863, and took charge of a colored congregation in Newark, where he died Aug. 19, 1865, unmarried.

Stanton, Rev. Robert P., is now pastor of the Congregational church at Greenville, Conn.

Willes, Rev. Daniel, E., is an Episcopal clergyman, and resides at Hobart, Albany county, N. Y.

Note G.

PHYSICIANS OF WEST FARMS, NOW FRANKLIN.

The medical profession in ancient Norwich was more than respectable; was distinguished. As practitioners, several of its members had few superiors in the country, and West Farms had her full proportion of men of ability. The first that we shall notice as coming under our observation, was

Dr. John Olmstead, or *Holmstead*, who came to Norwich from Saybrook with the colony of settlers in 1660, and was classed as one of the Original Proprietors. Though originally located at the Town Plot, he was, for a considerable time, the sole physician of the settlement at West Farms. He was something of a surgeon, and is said to have had considerable skill in the treatment of wounds, particularly those caused

by the bite of the rattlesnake. He was fond of frontier life and enjoyed
in a high degree the sports of the chase. He died in 1686.

Dr. Solomon Tracy was the next physician in the order of time.
He was the fifth son of Lieut. Thomas, and came to Norwich in 1660 with
his father, at the age of nine years. When of suitable age he was in-
structed in the healing art by Dr. Olmstead, and located in business at
the Town Plot. As his elder brother, John, had settled at West Farms,
he was drawn thither, and for a considerable time was the sole physician
in this section. He died July 9, 1732.

Dr. David Hartshorne was the earliest physician who actually settled
at Norwich West Farms. Dr. Hartshorne was born in Reading, Massachusetts, 1656. He first located in business in his native town, where
he continued till about the year 1700, when he removed to this place.
In his new field of labor he was highly esteemed as a physician, and was
a leading man both in civil and ecclesiastical affairs. He was also one of
the original deacons of the church, and generally held in trust the funds
of the society. Dr. Hartshorne died November 3d, 1738.

Dr. Robert Bell, from Ipswich, father-in-law of Capt. John Fillmore,
was a cotemporary of Dr. Hartshorne, and was located near the present
village of Baltic. He died Aug. 23, 1727.

Dr. John Sabin was born in Pomfret, Windham county, Connecticut, 1696. Removing early to Portapaug, he acquired an extensive
practice. Upon his tombstone it is stated that he was captain of one
of the Norwich foot companies. The fact that he was several times
deputed as agent to transact important business with the legislature,
shows that he was held in estimation. He married for second wife,
Nov. 3d, 1730, Hannah Starr, of Dedham ; died March 2d, 1742.
Dr. Sabin was the ancestor of Hon. LaFayette S. Foster, U. S. Senator from Connecticut and Vice President of the Senate.

Dr. Thomas Worden should certainly be noticed as among the early
physicians at West Farms. He was a son of Samuel Worden, read
medicine with Dr. Hartshorne, and resided upon the hillside a short distance south-west from the village of Baltic. Although his advantages
were slender and his location obscure, and although his death occurred
more than a century ago, (1759,) yet his name has been handed down
to our own time in connection with a prescription which he originally
used in his practice. Dec. 17, 1728, the town voted to Dr. Thomas
Worden " for travel and Medisons applied to Ebenezer Hunter's child,
3."

As indicating the public solicitude early manifested for the unfortunate poor, we add a few items from the records.—

"Jan. 4, 1726-7, voted to allow Dr. David Hartshorne, for services to Gaylor, £o. 7s. od."

"To Thomas Blythe, for tending Gaylor, £2. 2s. od."

"To 13 watchers with Gaylor, 2s. each per night, £2. 2s. od."

December 19, 1727, "To Thomas Blythe, for digging Gaylor's grave, £o. 5s. od."

July 5, 1727, "The inhabitants do now by their vote, agree to allow to each man that watches with Micah Rood, two shillings per night. Also to those who have attended said Rood by the day, three shillings per day."

"Dec. 17, 1728, to Jacob Hyde, for digging Micah Rood's grave, £o. 4s. od."

Dr. Theophilus Rogers was born at Lynn, Massachusetts, October 4th, 1699, the sixth in descent from John Rogers, the proto-martyr, who was burned at Smithfield, February 4th, 1555. Dr. Rogers studied his profession, and practiced for a while, in Boston. Afterwards he removed to Norwich West Farms, where he entered upon a wide sphere of usefulness. Dr. Roger's name has come down to us in connection with striking eccentricities. While he possessed firmness and good judgment as a physician, his natural timidity was excessive. It is said that he built his house, which is still standing, [the residence of the late Jason W. Kingsley] very low between joints in order to avoid danger from high winds, and covered the windows with wooden shutters, to keep out the glare of lightning. Whenever called abroad in the night, he preferred to have some one accompany him. He died Sept. 29, 1753. His wife died on the 17th of November, of the same year, and both sleep in one grave.

Dr. Ezekiel Rogers, eldest son of the above, was born October 2, 1723. Talented and amiable, he entered upon his professional career with bright prospects. But the hopes of many friends were doomed to disappointment, for in the flower of youth he died, Nov. 11, 1745.

Dr. John Barker, whose residence was located in the eastern part of the West Farms Society, was the eldest son of John and Hannah (Brewster) Barker, and was born in Lebanon, Connecticut, in 1729. The ordinary school advantages of that day he carefully improved. As a medical student in the office of Dr. Joseph Perkins, his close application, keen insight into the mysteries of disease, and particularly his quick and accurate interpretation of equivocal symptoms, gave certain promise of future success. Commencing business in 1750, he labored in the same field for more than forty years, till stricken down by sudden death. As a physician, Dr. Barker enjoyed an enviable popularity, both with the public and the profession. He was extensively employed in consultation throughout eastern Connecticut, and great deference was yielded to his opinions.

He was one of the original memorialists who petitioned the legislature for a medical society. Not discouraged by that attempt, he and his compeers persevered till, ten or twelve years later, their efforts resulted in the organization of a voluntary association, with Dr. Barker for its first President. To this position he was annually re-elected so long as he lived.

Many anecdotes of Dr. Barker are still preserved. For these we have no room. But even without collateral evidence, these would show that he was a man of sparkling wit, quick perceptions, sound common sense, and not least, generous heart. It was to these strong and noble traits of character that he owed his success, for he was not graced with elegance of person or polish of manner, nor did his pointed repartees derive their force from any fastidious selection of words. His careless and slovenly habits led a cotemporary to remark,—

> "Barker, a diamond, was both coarse and rough,
> But yet a diamond was, of sterling worth."

He died June 13, 1791, of cholera morbus. On the 19th of September following, Dr. Philemon Tracy, by appointment, delivered a eulogy on his life and character, before the New London Co. Medical Society.

Dr. Obadiah Kingsbury, son of Ephraim Kingsbury, was born at West Farms, 1735. He studied with Dr. Barker, and located in his native parish. Though dying in 1776, at an early age, he accumulated, by his industry, a handsome estate.

Dr. Nathaniel Hyde was born at West Farms, 1746, and was the fourth son of Abner Hyde. He studied with Dr. Barker, who had married his sister, and located in West Farms near the residence of the late Tommy Hyde. He was a judicious practitioner, though his remedies were chiefly of a domestic character. His field of labor was limited, and he had abundant leisure, which was devoted to reading and meditation. The English classics were his favorite field, and he could recite the whole of Paradise Lost from memory. He is said to have done most of his business on foot. Dr. Hyde never married; died 1832.

Dr. Benjamin Ellis, son of Rev. John Ellis, was born at West Farms, 1752. He studied with Dr. Joshua Downer of Preston, and settling at West Farms, acquired an extensive practice, particularly in the department of obstetrics. Dr. Ellis died in 1825.

Dr. Elijah Hartshorne was born at West Farms, 1754. He studied with Dr. Phillip Turner, and located in the southern part of his native society. Dr. Hartshorne was a careful and judicious practitioner. His field was a circumscribed one, and he did his business on foot. His death occurred in 1839.

These three cotemporaries were succeeded by *Dr. Reuben Burgess*, who died in 1833.

The Writer located in Franklin, in 1829, and has been the sole practitioner of the place since 1833.

Thus much for the resident physicians of Franklin. We subjoin brief notices of those natives of Franklin who have located as physicians in other places :—

Dr. Christopher Huntington was the eldest son of Christopher, of West Farms, and grandson of Christopher, the first male child born in Norwich. Dr. Huntington located in Bozrah, and appears to have been the sole physician of New Concord, during its early history; died in 1800.

He married, September 29, 1748, Sarah Bingham, and had six children, of whom the youngest, Christopher, became a physician.

Dr. Theophilus Rogers, Jr., was the son of Dr. Theophilus Rogers, of West Farms, with whom he studied his professson. He located at Bean Hill. The labors of an extensive practice, he performed, according to the usual custom, on horseback. In the revolution, Dr. Rogers was a staunch whig, a member of the committee of safety, and very active in the cause of liberty.

He married, March 25, 1754, Penelope Jarvis, of Roxbury, and had one son and three daughters. He died, September 29, 1801, aged 70. He was noted for rigid adherence to etiquette and nicety in matters of dress and appearance. Habitual courtesy, graceful manners, and skill in the winsome play of conversation, threw a charm around his presence which was felt alike by young and old.

The name and family have been distinguished in both the medical and clerical professions, on each side of the Atlantic.

Dr. Elisha Tracy, son of Captain Joseph Tracy, was born at West Farms, in 1712, and graduated at Yale College in 1738. It was the wish of his friends that he should enter the ministry, but yielding to his own predelictions, he commenced the study of medicine under the direction of Dr. Theophilus Rogers, Sen., and settled in business in Norwich. He possessed thorough classical scholarship, and was well versed in medical literature.

In 1775, Dr. Tracy was appointed one of the members of a committee to examine all candidates applying for situations in the army, either as surgeons or assistant surgeons.

For his earnest advocacy of inoculation for small pox, he encountered a storm of prejudice and persecution. By two grand jurors of the county he was presented "for communicating the small pox, by inoculation, to Elijah Lathrop and Benjamin Ward, both of Norwich, aforesaid, and sundry other persons, against the peace, and contrary to the laws of this state." Pleading guilty to the charge, he was held in a recognizance of sixty pounds, to appear and answer before the county court. He was fortunate, however, in living to see his own views very generally adopted by the community.

Dr. Tracy was the author of the inscription in memory of Samuel Uncas,* that brought to light the obscure Indian word, " Wauregan," which has since acquired great local popularity.

After an active life of forty-five years, he died, in 1783, widely beloved and lamented.

Dr. Samuel H. Barker, son of Dr. John Barker, born at West Farms, in 1753, studied medicine with his father, and located in business at Lebanon Crank, now Columbia, where he died, June 11, 1794, much lamented.

In an obituary notice by one of his pupils, we find the following :—

> " If worth and merit from death's jaws could save,
> Barker, our friend, had always shunned the grave."

Dr. Phineas Hyde, son of Phineas Hyde and maternal grandson of Dr. Theophilus Rogers, was born at West Farms, 1749. He practiced successively at Poquetanock and Mystic. During the Revolution he was a surgeon in the service both in the army and navy. He died in 1820.

---

* The epitaph is as follows :—

> " For beauty, wit, for sterling sense,
> For temper mild, for eloquence,
> For courage bold, for things wauregan,
> He was the glory of Moheagan—
> Whose death has caused great lamentation
> Both in ye English and ye Indian nation."

Dr. Luther Waterman was born at West Farms about 1750. He married Jerusha, daughter of his preceptor, Dr. Barker. He was attached as surgeon to the forces under Colonel Knowlton, during the campaign of 1776. After the war he removed to the west.

Dr. Gurdon Huntington, son of Dea. Barnabas, was born at West Farms, in 1768. His preliminary studies were under the direction of his pastor, Rev. Samuel Nott, and in medicine he was the pupil of Dr. Lord. He located in business at Unadilla, N. Y., where he died, July 13, 1847.

Dr. Asher Huntington, son of Ezra, was born at West Farms, Feb. 25, 1770. He studied medicine under the direction of Dr. Philemon Tracy, and commenced practice in Preston, Conn., but not very long afterwards removed to Chenango, N. Y., where he died, in 1833.

Dr. Abel Huntington was born at West Farms, 1777. He located at East Hampton, Long Island, was a member of the New York senate, and from 1833 to 1837 represented his district in congress, besides filling other offices from time to time, and always worthily. Died, 1858.

NOTE H.

Biographical sketches of individuals not included in the clerical or medical professions.

Foster, LaFayette S., LL.D., was born at Franklin, Nov. 22d, 1806, being a direct descendant of the famous Capt. Miles Standish, and also a lineal descendant of Doctor John Sabin, an early physician at West Farms. He graduated at Brown University in 1828; became a lawyer by profession, and located in business in Norwich, where he now resides. He was a member of the General Assembly of Connecticut for six sessions, between 1839 and 1854, during three of which he was Speaker of the House; was Mayor of the city of Norwich several years, and was chosen a senator in congress for a term of six years from March 4, 1855. Having been re-elected to that office, he remained in the senate for a period of twelve years, during the last two of which he was President of that body, and acting Vice President of the United States, and in the event of a vacancy would have become President by virtue of his office. He has recently been elected to the Professorship of Law, in Yale College.

Fillmore, Hon. Millard, eldest son of Nathaniel Fillmore, and great-grandson of Captain John Fillmore, (of whom a brief notice has already been given,) was born, Jan. 7, 1800, not in Franklin, but Summer Hill, N. Y. Though not a native of Franklin, the Fillmore family has so long resided in this locality, and been so identified with its history, that by common consent we claim this distinguished individual as belonging to us.

At the age of nineteen years he commenced the study of law, and four years later was admitted to the bar and entered upon his professional career at Aurora, N. Y. His political life commenced with his election to the State Assembly in 1829, at about which period he removed to Buffalo, where he now resides. In 1832, he was elected to Congress, and continued to hold a seat in the national legislature, with one or two short interruptions, till 1843, when he declined a re-election. In 1847 he was elected to the office of Comptroller of the State, and the next year was nominated by the whig party as their candidate for Vice President, and was elected to that office in the autumn following. In March, 1849, he assumed the duties of his new position, where he remained till the death of President Taylor, in July, 1850, by which event he was elevated to the presidential chair. His term of office expired in 1853, after which he retired from public life.

Hyde, Lieut. Governor Ephraim H., was born at Stafford, Conn. He is a lineal descendant of the first Thomas Hyde of West Farms, now Franklin, who was of the third generation from William the Proprietor. Gov. Hyde's tastes naturally incline to agriculture, and he has devoted the greater part of his life to this pursuit. He has probably been the pioneer of scientific agriculture in this state. He was one of the earliest breeders of Durham stock, and in 1851 began to breed the celebrated Devon stock, and is now the largest breeder in New England, if not in the United States. When Gov. Hyde began breeding imported stock, the sentiment of farmers generally was strongly against it. But, with one or two associates, he persevered, and soon fully established the superiority of the new animals. It is not too much to say that this demonstration of the capabilities of stock culture has revolutionized the ideas, if not yet the practice, of the entire farming community of the state. Gov. Hyde also early advocated a greater application of scientific knowledge to the culture of crops, and has been an earnest worker in this field, where the majority of our farmers strangely reject the aid which science stands ready to offer. He was one of a few who received a charter for the Conn. State Agricultural Society, in 1852, and has been connected with the Society in an official capacity since its organization, and since 1859, as president.

Yours Very Truly
Ephm H. Hyde

He was also active in securing the organization of the State Board of Agriculture, in 1866, and has been Vice President of the Board from the first. He was also zealous in forming the Tolland Co. Agricultural Society, and has been its chief officer for a majority of the years.

Gov. Hyde is not an active politician, though he has often been called to political office. He was several times the representative of Stafford in the legislature, and in 1867 was elected Lieutenant Governor of the State, to which office he was re-elected the following year.

Kingsbury, Col. Jacob, was born at Norwich West Farms, June 6, 1756, and was a great-grandson of Joseph Kingsbury, Sr., one of the first deacons of the West Farms church. This ancestor was a resident at Haverhill, Mass., at the time of the Indian massacre in 1708, whence, in June of the same year, he removed with his wife, Love (Ayer,) to West Farms. We may presume that he was drawn hither by the influence of the veteran, John Ayer, a kinsman of his wife. On the maternal side Col. Kingsbury was descended from Gen. Daniel Dennison, Gov. Thomas Dudley and Sir Richard Saltonstall, prominent members of the early colonies.

The ringing call that sounded from Concord over the land, met a quick response from him, and he at once hastened to join the army at Roxbury, and enlisted in the company commanded by his cousin, Capt. Asa Kingsbury. He remained constantly in service, and was, in 1780, commissioned ensign, in which capacity he served till the end of the war. At its close he was promoted to a Lieutenantcy, and assigned to the western army, where he continued uninterruptedly for fourteen years. During the last nine years of this period, to use his own words, he was " not absent from military duty one hour." This frontier service in those days of ambuscades and massacres, when the posts were weak and widely separated, but the foe numerous and ever on the alert, was one of the greatest toil and danger. Ceaseless vigilance was the only price of safety. He here received the well earned promotions of Captain and Major. The following General Order bears witness to the soldierly qualities of Lieut. Kingsbury, and well illustrates the exigencies of the early border service.

FORT WASHINGTON, 14th January, 1791.

Extract of General Orders :

The General is highly pleased with the cool and spirited conduct displayed by Lieutenant Kingsbury in repulsing a body of about 300 savages, who surrounded Dunlap's station on Monday morning last and besieged it, endeavoring to set it on fire with their arrows, and keeping up a heavy fire against his small party for the space of twenty-five hours. * * * * * * This spirited defence made by Lieut. Kingsbury, with so small a force as 35 men total, old and young, sick and well, and in such bad works, reflects the greatest credit upon him and his party. The General returns his thanks to him, and directs that the Adjutant transmit him a copy of these orders by the first conveyance.

JOS. HARMAR, *Brig. General.*

In 1799 he returned to Connecticut upon a furlough, where he spent the two following years in the recruiting service, and married his wife, Miss Sally P. Ellis. But in 1802, he was again ordered to the frontier, and stationed among the Creek Indians, in Georgia. Toward the close of the following year he was appointed Lieut. Colonel, and transferred to the western army, whence he was shortly transferred to the south-western army, where he remained for several years, and in 1809 became Colonel. His services in the south-west covered the years in which Aaron Burr figured largely in that section. Burr called several times at the headquarters of Col. Kingsbury, and was evidently anxious to enlist his sympathies. But the two never met. Col. Kingsbury regarded him with suspicion, and was unwilling to compromise his own honor by intercourse with him.

Very early in the war of 1812, Col. Kingsbury was stationed at Detroit, and, as he once stated to the writer, was offered the command at that post which subsequently devolved upon Gen. Hull, and which he himself could not accept, as he was unable to leave his quarters on account of sickness. He was afterwards assigned to the command of Fort Adams, in Newport harbor. While in command at this post, he was appointed Inspector General of the New England forces, in which capacity he served till the close of the war, when he retired to his home in Franklin. He died at Franklin, July 1, 1837.

Colonel Kingsbury was a man of unswerving honor and integrity, and followed unflinchingly the path of duty. These qualities were strikingly exemplified throughout the nearly fifty years of his military life, and won for him universal respect and esteem. In the Senate of the United States, Gen. William H. Harrison, mentioning him as the first Captain under whom he served, truly remarked, that neither " Rome nor Sparta ever produced a better soldier."

Mason, Jeremiah, LL.D., was born at Lebanon Conn., April 27, 1768, but his father and several of his elder sisters were born at West

Farms, at the old family mansion. He was the second son of Col. Jeremiah Mason, and a lineal descendant of Major John Mason. Destined for an education and for professional life, he entered Yale College, where he graduated with high honors in 1788. After devoting several years to study in the law office of the Hon. Stephen Rowe Bradley, of Vermont, he was admitted to the bar in that state in 1791, and shortly afterwards commenced his professional career at Walpole, N. H., but was soon inclined by his rapidly growing popularity to seek a broader field for practice, and removed to Portsmouth in the same State, where he became the personal and, as the event proved, life-long friend of Daniel Webster. In 1802 he was appointed Attorney General of that State, and from 1813 to 1817 was a leading member of the United States Senate, but resigned his seat for the purpose of devoting himself more exclusively to his profession, in which he was profoundly learned, particularly in the department of common law.

He removed to Boston in 1832, where he died in 1848. He will be remembered by many as the learned and successful advocate of Rev. Ephraim K. Avery, when on trial for the murder of Sarah Maria Cornell.

Tracy, Hon. Uriah, son of Eliphalet and great-grandson of John Tracy, the Proprietor, was born at West Farms, Feb. 2, 1755. Being destined for professional life he entered Yale College, where he graduated in 1778; afterwards read law in Litchfield; settled in that town, and soon rose to eminence in his profession. He often represented his town in the State Legislature, and in 1793 was Speaker of the House. He was a representative in Congress from 1793 to 1796, and from that time onward to 1807 was a leading member of the United States Senate, and a part of the time President pro. tem. of that branch of Congress. He was also a Major-General of militia, and is said to have been an instructive and agreeable companion. He died at the national capitol, July 19, 1807, and was the first to be interred in the congressional burying ground.

Note I.

We append a list of missionaries raised up in Franklin. As the lists heretofore published have been more or less inaccurate, we extend the present list so as to embrace the whole of the original town of Norwich.

Year.	Name.	Mission.
1761—Rev. Samson Occum,		Oneida.
1766—Rev. Samuel Kirtland,		Oneida.
1771—Rev. David Avery,		Oneida.
1795—Rev. Eliphalet Nott, D. D.,		Central New York.
1806—Rev. John Churchill Rudd, D D.,		Long Island.
1812—Rev. Samuel Nott, Jr.,		Mahratta.
1812—Mrs. Nott, (Roxana Peck,)		Mahratta.
1812—Rev. Eli Hyde,		Northern New York.
1819—Rev. Miron Winslow,		Ceylon.
1819—Mrs. Winslow, (Harriet L. Lathrop,)		Ceylon.
1820—Rev. William Potter,		Cherokee.
1825—Rev. William H. Manwaring,		Cherokee.
1826—Rev. Anson Gleason,		Choctaw.
1826—Mrs. Gleason, (B. W. Tracy,)		Choctaw.
1827—Mrs. Gulic, (Fanny H. Thomas,)		Sandwich Islands.
1827—Mrs. Eli Smith, (Sarah L. Huntington,)		Syria.
1835—Mrs. Perry, (Harriet L. Lathrop,)		Ceylon.
1835—Rev. James T. Dickinson,		Singapore.
1836—Rev. William Tracy,		Madura.
1836—Mrs. Cherry, (Charlotte H. Lathrop,)		Madura.
1839—Mrs. Brewer, (Laura L. Giddings,)		Oregon.
1839—Mrs. Cherry, (Jane E. Lathrop,)		Ceylon.
1840—Rev. Joshua Smith,		Africa.
1844—Miss Lucinda Downer,		Choctaw.
1844—Miss Susan Tracy,		Choctaw.
1848—Mrs. C. C. Copeland, (Cornelia Ladd,)		Choctaw.
1849—Miss Eunice Starr,		Choctaw.
1852—Miss Elizabeth Backus,		Choctaw.
1852—Mrs. H. B. Haskell, (Sarah J. Brewster,)		Assyrian Mission.
1852—Rev. Nathan L. Lord, M. D.,		Ceylon.
1855—Rev. William Aitchison,		China.
1860—Rev. William F. Arms,		Bulgaria.

Note J.

THE PORTIPAUG, OR NORWICH EIGHTH SOCIETY.

A history of West Farms, or the second society in Norwich, would evidently be incomplete without further allusion to the ecclesiastical history of the eighth society, and a brief sketch of that organization will now be attempted. We have seen that a bitter sectional controversy existed in the second society for a period of about twenty years, during which time the second church edifice was erected, near the site of the first, in the face of fierce and constant opposition; the factious minority adding to their other opposition, threats of separation, and frequently petitioning the society and General Assembly to that effect. At length, both parties having tired of agitation, it was voted in society meeting, in 1758, "that a number of inhabitants in the north-east part of the Society have leave to withdraw and form a separate organization." This action of the society was confirmed in 1761, when what was originally the north-eastern section of the second, became the eighth society in Norwich. The boundary lines were essentially the same as those that have existed in our own day. The eighth society held its first meeting, June 29, 1761, at which Capt. Jacob Hyde was chosen Moderator, William Brett, Clerk, and Capt. Jacob Hyde, Capt. Benajah Sabin and Capt. John Fillmore, a committee.

As the individuals constituting the disaffected party counted upon a final separation as only a question of time, they were careful to secure the material composing the first church edifice when it was removed to make room for the second. This was subsequently erected upon a rise of ground a short distance south-east of the residence of Austin Ladd, upon the opposite side of the highway. A church evidently had been organized, which adopted the peculiarities of the Separatists of that day, a number of years anterior to the legal division of the society; for, as early as Oct. 29, 1746, Thomas Denison was ordained their pastor, which office he continued to hold for about twelve years. This Thomas Denison is said to have been the owner of the ground upon which this first meeting house was erected. Within one month after its organization, July 21st, 1761, the society voted "to concur with the church in extending an invitation to Rev. Isaac Foster to settle in the work of the gospel ministry among us on the conditions mentioned in the warning." This vote was rescinded January 19th, 1762. But outside troubles have hardly ceased before domestic feuds threaten still greater difficulty. On the 11th of June, 1762, the society find it necessary to join with the church in mutual council concerning the difficulties existing in their midst, and also to invoke the arbitration of the General Association.

On the 12th of September, 1763, the vote of invitation to Rev. Isaac Foster to become their pastor was renewed, and a committee was appointed to repair to Harvard and Ipswich, Mass., where Mr. Foster had formerly resided, to enquire concerning his moral character. The investigations of their committee resulted in a second rescission of the invitation to Mr. Foster*.

It was next voted, May 9th, 1764, to invite some licensed orthodox candidate that hath been liberally educated, to preach the gospel in said society. Soon afterwards, Rev. Joseph Denison was employed for a number of Sabbaths to supply the pulpit. Mr. Denison had graduated at Yale College the year previous and stood well with the Separates. This might have led to his employment here. For the succeeding two years quite a number of young men were employed to temporarily supply the pulpit rather than as candidates for settlement. Of the number may be mentioned Reverends James Treadway, Ambrose Collens, Ephraim Judson, Abner Johnson and Thomas Welles Bray, all of them recent graduates of Yale College,—also Rev. Joseph Lee, a graduate of Harvard. It is thus evident that they were in favor of an educated ministry.

In 1766, Rev. Jesse Ives, also a graduate of Yale, was invited to preach, on probation, and subsequently settled as their minister with an annual salary of ninety-five pounds, one half in money and the remainder in provisions. To this sum was added thirty cords of good fire wood delivered at the door of his dwelling. Although Mr. Ives was the only settled pastor ever enjoyed by the eighth society as such, his ministry was of short duration, for in 1770 his salary was withheld by a vote of the society, and shortly afterwards he removed to Monson, Mass.

At this period the church, which partook largely of the Separate element, became very feeble, and ere long, it is said, ceased to exist as a distinct organization. And although the society had early manifested an earnest purpose by its oft repeated votes to supply the stated ministrations of the gospel, their zeal had so declined that in 1784 a vote was passed to dispose of the meeting house to raise the sum of four pounds, lawful money, to pay the remaining liability of the society to Rev. Jesse Ives. Two years later, May, 1786, this eighth society in

---

* It is not stated what the charges were that were preferred against Mr Foster. He received an honorary degree of A. M. from Yale College in 1739, and from Dartmouth in 1778. He died in 1794.

Norwich became the second society in Franklin. It retained a nominal organization by meeting annually at private dwellings for the choice of society officers, till the close of the last century, and perhaps somewhat later, but this community does not appear to have enjoyed, during this period, any considerable religious privileges. In 1798 an initial movement was made in the right direction, to which reference will again be made.

If the society, as an ecclesiastical organization, was barely possessed of vitality sufficient to keep it in being, it did not fail to exert a salutary influence upon the four school districts within its limits. These were respectively called the "Jockey Island," or 1st district, "Portipaug," or 2d, "Woodtown," or 3d, and "Great Hill," or the 4th. These were solely under its charge and supervision, and it is believed that the society herein faithfully discharged its obligations to the community. The society also voted in 1767 to instruct the committee to treat with Capt. Benajah Sabin for a plot of land for a burying ground. This purchase was to enlarge a plot where graves had already been opened. It was again enlarged in 1792. This cemetery, the only one now in use in this section of the town, has recently been enlarged and greatly improved. The church, which was taken down and sold to Comfort Fillmore, in 1784, and which was used by him in the construction of his dwelling, was substantially the same building that had, at an earlier period, stood upon Meeting House Hill, and parts of this same rude edifice were brought to Meeting House Hill from the Town Plot where they had originally been used in constructing an early church in that locality.

It will thus appear that the same building materials which constituted an important part of the meeting house built by John Elderkin, at the Town Plot in 1673, entered somewhat largely into the first church built upon Meeting House Hill more than forty years subsequent to that date. This, in turn, was taken down and re-erected in 1746, in what was afterwards the eighth society in Norwich, and after battling with the elements for nearly forty years longer, it had to succumb a third time, and parts of it were finally converted into a dwelling house, where very possibly some remnants may be found at the present time.

But a day of more promise is destined to dawn upon this community, for in 1798, a committee was appointed to select a site for another meeting house. This committee reported in favor of the corner of land then belonging to the Fox heirs, over against the dwelling of Josiah Tracy, 3d, and that one acre of land should be secured. This move resulted in a free church that was erected here a few years later by the voluntary contributions of individuals.* The seats were not only to be free, but the pulpit was to be open for all denominations of christians. Before this house was ready for use, and perhaps for a considerable time anterior to that period, public worship had been more or less regluarly held at private dwellings on the Sabbath.

Although, as already stated, the pulpit was to be open for all denominations, it was almost uniformly and uninterruptedly improved by the Methodists till the village of Baltic sprung up upon the eastern border of the town. After the incorporation of the town of Sprague, in 1861, which included within its limits a large portion of the original eighth society, a new center was not only formed for business, but for public worship on the Sabbath also. As a result, the meeting house which had been statedly occupied on the Sabbath for more than forty years, was deserted, and finally removed and its foundations razed to the earth.

---

* This church was completed in 1815. About thirty years afterwards, (in 1844,) the late Bailey Ayer generously presented the society with the means for procuring a bell. After this bell had pealed forth its familiar sounds from the church tower for one-fourth of a century, and after it had ceased to be heard in its original locality, it was secured by the committee of the first society and transferred to the church on the Hill, where it now regularly breaks the stillness of each returning Sabbath.

Historical Sermon,

BY

Rev. Franklin C. Jones.

The Historical Address was followed by the singing of
the anthem, "Blessed are the people." The pastor, Rev.
FRANKLIN C. JONES, then delivered the following

HISTORICAL SERMON.

—— •◆• ——

The history of the Ecclesiastical Society in this place,
already presented, prepares us the better to understand
the internal history of the church itself. To sketch the
leading features of this history is the object of the present
discourse.

An appropriate motto for this historic epitome occurs
in Isaiah 49 : 16—" BEHOLD, I HAVE GRAVEN THEE UPON
THE PALMS OF MY HANDS; THY WALLS ARE CONTINUALLY
BEFORE ME."

These words beautifully express the constancy of Jeho-
vah's care for his church. It is the object of his unceasing
regard. By day and by night, from generation to generation and from age to age He watches it for its safety
and seeks its prosperity. The history of the church
universal is a continuous illustration of these words.
And not only so, but each branch of that vine which is to
overshadow all the earth enjoys his fostering care. Every
particular church lives and grows through the centuries,
because its name is engraven before God. Its strength is
not in the skill and courage of the men who line its
battlements, but in the Almighty, who has its walls continually before him. Its members are ever dying, but the
church lives on. The aged oak of our woods is to-day

preparing to shed its foliage; and so it has done in each succeeding autumn for centuries. Yet it is the same oak whose dry leaves were driven before the November blast, when the Pequot and Mohegan still roamed a pathless wilderness. Four generations of the members of this church have lived and passed away; but the spiritual organism to which they belonged still lives, and we of the fifth generation are united to all who have gone before us, by our membership in this living body. He who founded has watched over it, and as we trace its life we should gratefully acknowledge his loving and faithful care.

The second Wednesday and eighth day of October, 1718,—one hundred and fifty years ago,—was an important day among the West Farmers of the town of Norwich. On that day their long cherished hope of having a church and a minister of their own was fulfilled. For at least eight years they had been waiting for a suitable time to accomplish this. They were people who loved the house of God; but as year after year they had plodded through mud or drifted snow, afoot or on horse-back, to worship in the meeting house on the town plot, they had deeply felt the desirableness of having a sanctuary more easily accessible, and a pastor who might more readily find and tend his flock. In the year 1716, as we have seen, a favorable opportunity had occurred for the formation of an ecclesiastical society. This was, to some extent, an experiment. When two years had elapsed, the people of the West Farms felt that they had demonstrated their ability to maintain a church and support a pastor among themselves. The necessary consent of the colonial government was obtained by a petition addressed to the General Court, assembled at Hartford in May, 1718. Mr. Henry Willes, of Windsor,—a graduate in 1715 of the college at

Saybrook, which was soon after to become Yale College at New Haven,—had been preaching to the people of West Farms for a year, and was ready to accede to their wish that he should be ordained as their minister.

On the eighth of October a church was formally organized[*] by the subscription of eight persons to a confession of faith, and these eight on the same day proceeded to ordain one of their number, Henry Willes, as their pastor. Of the composition of the council, or the religious exercises connected with these acts, we know nothing. It is quite probable that among the ministers present on this occasion were James Noyes, who had been forty-four years pastor of the church in Stonington, and who was then much the oldest pastor in eastern Connecticut; Eliphalet Adams, of New London; Ephraim Woodbridge, of Groton; Salmon Treat, of Preston; Samuel Whiting, of Windham, and Joseph Parsons, of Lebanon. There was one, however, of whose presence on that day we may be almost sure, namely, the Rev. Benjamin Lord, the new and youthful pastor of the parent church of Norwich. He must have been a college companion of Mr. Willes, having graduated one year before him, and it is quite likely that through his instrumentality Mr. Willes had first been invited to address the little congregation at the West Farms. We cannot but regret that no record remains of the religious exercises on the day we commemorate. Perhaps it matters little. If a tree lives and bears good fruit, the inquiry by whom it was set out is comparatively unimportant. Yet we should be glad to

---

* The original records of the Ecclesiastical Society give the date of Mr. Willes' ordination as Oct. 8th. It is not positively known that the church was organized on the same day, but there are various reasons for believing that such was the case.

know who planted the tree under whose spreading boughs we gather to-day.

Eight women joined the new church by letter, probably on the very day of its organization, making in all sixteen members. Compared with the nearly nine hundred members who have since belonged to this church, this seems a small beginning. But it is not the part of the wise man to despise the day of small things. In the living acorn is enwrapped the oak. Doubtless the fathers who formed here the church of Christ felt that they were laying a foundation for many generations. They were like men who plant an orchard and think that their children and grandchildren will eat of its fruit when they are in their graves. There might have been those who said of this little church planted in a wilderness yet unsubdued, " Even that which they build, if a fox go up, he shall even break down their stone wall." The work, however, was not of men, but of God; the name of this church in the wilderness was graven before him, and in his keeping it has stood and prospered.

The Confession of Faith adopted by the infant church is a clearly and carefully worded document. Its Calvinism is neither " moderate " nor " consistent," but of the highest and strictest type. The language of the Westminster Assembly's Catechism is frequently quoted, and occasionally that of the Confession of 1680. On the subject of church government but little is said, and that little does not enable us to determine whether the sentiment of the new organization accorded with that prevailing in the parent church, which rejected the Saybrook platform.

The ministry of Mr. Willes embraces a period of thirtytwo years, closing in 1750. Excepting the last six years, it seems to have been a time of prosperity and peaceful

growth The church commenced its existence in a season
of great religious declension throughout the New England
colonies. A hundred years had elapsed since the first
settlement of New England. The religious faith and zeal
which animated the Pilgrims, were wanting among many
of their descendants. Many followed them to the New
World whose motives were less pure and elevated. While
the churches had, perhaps, lost nothing of the form of
orthodoxy in doctrine, some of them had lost much of the
power of godliness. The union of church and state, and
the extensive adoption of the "half-way covenant," had
diminished the purity of many churches, and broken down
the barriers which must ever divide the true people of
God from the world. Revivals of religion were rare and
of very limited extent. At such a time was this church
founded, and, so far as we can now judge, it enjoyed a
remarkable degree of spiritual prosperity in its early
years, being blessed with more frequent revivals of religion than many older churches of the colony. For a period
of twenty-six years, from its organization to 1744, not a
year passed without additions to its number on profession
of faith. During that time there were three periods of
special religious interest. The first was in 1721. In that
year there occurred a remarkably precious and powerful
revival in Windham, under the ministry of the Rev.
Samuel Whiting, in which eighty persons were added to
the church in that town. This work of grace was the
more remarkable from the general religious declension
throughout this region. The influence of that work seems
to have extended into the town of Norwich, and both the
First Church and that of West Farms shared its happy
fruits.

The movement known as the "Great Awakening"
appears to have begun as early as 1735, though the new

interest in religion did not become general until some
years later. In that year there were revivals of marked
interest and power in several churches, and among them
was the church in this place. This fact is significant of
the earnestness and pastoral fidelity of its minister. As
the result of this work of grace, thirty-one were added
to the church.

Six years later, at a time when the Spirit of God was
extensively poured out over the whole land, the church
was blessed with a revival more extensive in its manifest
results than any other ever enjoyed in this community.
Within the space of a little more than one year (1741–42),
one hundred persons united with it on profession of faith.
During the progress of this work the strength of Mr.
Willes gave way, and he was prostrated for several weeks
by sickness. But other trials more grievous than bodily
illness were in store for him. He was to see the peaceful
growth of the church stayed by controversies, partly
religious and partly secular. A period of nearly forty
years now passed, in which, from causes both internal and
external, the promise of its early years was interrupted.
The secular causes which led to the division of the church,
and afterwards of the society, have been already detailed.
But, as is usual in such cases, various influences conspired
to produce the result. It has been often remarked that
there is nothing about which men will fight so obstinately as
matters of religious belief and observance. The truth of
this saying was illustrated in this place a little more than
a hundred years ago.

It is well known that the good accomplished by the
revivals of the Great Awakening was not unmixed with
evil. There was much of fanatical excitement and extravagance. Violent outcries and bodily contortions were
supposed by many to be legitimate signs of the presence

of the Holy Spirit. A class of ignorant and noisy lay preachers arose, who declaimed against the ministry, and aimed only to excite the feelings and passions of their auditors. These disorders were lamented and opposed by Edwards and others of the wisest leaders of the work of reformation, as well as by the regular ministry in general. Some of the clergy were led to look with suspicion on the whole work, because of the disorders attending it. Others acknowledged the agency of the Spirit, while they also held that He could not be the author of confusion and extravagance. Of this class seem to have been Mr. Willes, the pastor of this church, and his early companion and life-long friend, Dr. Lord, of the First church in Norwich. In each of these churches, however, there was a party who espoused the views of those known as Separates or Separatists,—a denomination who professed to hold purer doctrine, and to be more strictly congregational in their government, than the regular churches. Many churches of this sect were formed in eastern Connecticut, by parties seceding from the established organizations; and among the churches thus divided were the First and Second of Norwich. That in this society was formed probably in 1746. Thomas Denison was ordained as its pastor in October of that year. But discord still prevailed in the church, which ultimately led to the dismission of Mr. Willes in 1750. He continued to reside here until his death in 1758. His funeral sermon was preached by Dr. Lord. Of the traits of his character or the details of his life we know but little. His name survives, and the general evidence that he was a faithful and successful minister. More than this,—and the best of all, —his work survives. The church which he aided in founding, and which grew under his pastoral care to such goodly proportions, still lives; and could we see all the

7

hidden channels of moral influence, as they lie before the Omniscient eye, we should doubtless perceive among us to-day agencies for good at work, which might be traced back to the labors of the first pastor of this church. The good man's work never dies. He may pass away; the spot where his dust reposes may be unknown; his very name may sink into oblivion, but his work lasts. The good which he has done is his everlasting memorial.

During a period of nearly three years following the dismission of Mr. Willes, the pulpit was supplied by various ministers, great pains being taken to hear none but orthodox preachers. In December, 1752, Mr. John Ellis, a native of Cambridge, Mass., and a graduate of Harvard college in the class of 1750, was invited to preach as a candidate. In February, 1753, he received a call to settle as pastor, the vote of the society in relation to it being fifty-eight in the affirmative and forty-nine in the negative. This record is sufficient evidence that dissensions still continued in the parish, and Mr. Ellis must have been a man of considerable resolution to accept the call under such circumstances. He was ordained in 1753, and held the office of pastor for twenty-six years. As he left no records, but little can now be known of the history of the church under his ministry. It was evidently not a peaceful or prosperous one. In the parish there was great discrepancy of views as to matters of doctrine and church government; and the excitement and financial embarrassment connected with the political condition of the country, was unfavorable to the prosperity of religion. Among the pastor's trials were those arising from extreme poverty, and the neglect or inability of the society to relieve his wants.

In this connection honorable mention should be made of the self-sacrificing patriotism of Mr. Ellis. He took a lively interest in the welfare of the country, and cheerfully shared with his people the burdens of war. In 1775 he relinquished one hundred pounds of his salary, in consideration, as he says in a letter still preserved, of the burdens which had come upon his people in aiding to fit out the expedition to Crown Point. In the Revolution also, Mr. Ellis warmly espoused the cause of independence, and entered the army as a chaplain in 1775. In this office he served until the conclusion of the war. Two of his sons also went into the army with him. With his enlistment in the public service his pastorate practically ceased, although the pastoral relation was not dissolved until 1779.

Although it was the lot of Mr. Ellis to labor in troublous times, and amid multiplied discouragements, not less than seventy persons were added to the church during his ministry,—a large number, if we consider the state of the church and of the country.

Another period of three years now passed, in which this flock was without a shepherd. We come down to the year 1782, in which our revolutionary struggle closed victoriously,—a year of hope and rejoicing throughout the land, and also one of auspicious omens for this parish. In March of that year a third pastor was ordained and installed over this church, whose ministry was destined to reach the almost unprecedented length of seventy years, whose name is still as ointment poured forth in this community, and whose influence will be seen and felt here for many years to come. It was high time that the vacant pastorate should be filled. The church had been, in effect, without a pastor during the whole period of the war. The Sabbath services had been much interrupted, the members of the church were scattered, and spiritual religion was at a low ebb. At this juncture there was

need of a minister earnest and energetic, to gather together
the scattered flock and rebuild the desolations of Zion.
Such an one was sent here in the person of SAMUEL NOTT,
a native of Saybrook, and a graduate of Yale College in
1780. He was licensed at Durham in 1781, and commenced preaching in this place in October of the same
year. His ordination occurred in March, 1782. From the
beginning he gave himself with characteristic energy to
the labors of the ministry. For several years after his
settlement his health was so feeble that no one would have
ventured to predict for him a long career. But his phys-
ical strength gradually improved, and during his long
ministry he was very rarely prevented by sickness from
the performance of official duty. That ministry was, from
the beginning, one of marked success. He has left interesting memoirs of it in two published sermons, whose
statements need not be recapitulated here. At the time
of his settlement the church numbered seventy-two. The
number received into it by him was four hundred and
twenty-seven. For forty years there was no very marked
revival of religion, but there were almost constant acces-
sions to the church. With Dr. Nott it seems to have
been always seed-time and always harvest. By the blessing of the Spirit he was ever reaping what he had sown
in earlier years, and ever sowing what he was to reap in
the years to come. The years 1821, 1831, and 1843, were
marked by special outpourings of the Spirit, and large
additions to the church.

Of Dr. Nott's characteristics as a man and a preacher,
it is difficult for one who had no personal acquaintance
with him to speak to those who were familiar with his
character and life. His image will rise vividly before the
minds of many of you who have gathered here to-day, as
associated with much that is most precious and most hal-

lowed in the memories of by-gone years. Here are those
to whom in infancy the seal of God's covenant was applied
by his hand; those who even in childhood learned to ven-
erate, and at the same time to love him; those who by
him were united in the sacred bonds of marriage; those
who at the funeral of many a loved one listened to his
words of instruction and sympathy; those who felt
honored in receiving him as a guest in their houses; those
who Sabbath after Sabbath were led by him to the throne
of grace, and heard the divine word clearly and faithfully
explained; some who went to him in periods of trial and
perplexity for counsel, and received sage advice, for which
they have never ceased to bless God and revere his servant; and many whose opinions and character to-day bear
the clear impress of his sound and faithful teachings.

As a man, Dr. Nott was distinguished for his energy
and decision of character. The circumstances in which
he obtained his education illustrate this. Until he was
twenty years old his life was passed in mechanical labor.
Then, with little to depend upon but his own exertions,
he resolved to secure an education; and through many
embarrassments he persevered until the end. So in his
ministry, whatever he did was done heartily and with a
will, and the momentum of his own determination carried
others along with him. For punctuality he might be
ranked with General Washington himself. He came and
went, began and ended by the clock, and expected others
to do the same.

He was a man of great industry. "One duty follows
another," was his motto, and he was ready for each duty
as it came round. He accomplished a larger amount of
labor than many others, because he kept doing while other
men were resting or deciding what to do. His working
power was increased by his remarkable cheerfulness of

spirit, the result both of his native temperament and of his christian faith. With unusual serenity of soul he passed through the many domestic and public trials appointed to him, maintaining habitually that rare qualification for usefulness, "a heart at leisure from itself." In addition to his ministerial labors and the cares of a large family, he gave instruction for many years to young men placed in his household. He fitted many for college, and not a few ministers received their theological training with him. Thus he became "a maker of public men."

He was a man of sound judgment, discreet in dealing with men, and in managing the affairs of his parish; possessing much of that common sense, which is often worth more than learning or eloquence, and without which the wisest will often play the fool; skilled in estimating men and things at their true value. He was also of a highly affectionate and social disposition, entering readily into the joys and sorrows of others, even to the last of life; and having a peculiar aptness in introducing religious themes in conversation. "He was a man," says Dr. McEwen, "whose social affections never wore out. Rarely has a very aged minister lived who, having buried his generation, could be so social, so happy, and so useful among survivors."

As a preacher, Dr. Nott has been thus described by one who was a native of this town and who knew him well. "His sermons were marked by great simplicity of thought and style, and were devoted to the inculcation of the great doctrines and duties of religion. He was not learned, but had a quick and strong sense, an imagination of sufficient power to illustrate his thoughts often by bold figures, and a tenderness and fervor of feeling that gave them a deep impression on his hearers. He never indulged in abstruse speculation, nor wasted his efforts on trifles. In the pulpit he was grave, dignified, earnest and impressive, and had eminently the air of an ambassador of God. When animated, his attitude and air often became commanding, and occasionally thoughts and emotions flashed from his lips that were strikingly beautiful and impressive. In prayer he was simple, pertinent, and fervid, and he read the Scriptures with unusual propriety and force."*

This church has great reason to bless God that such a man was given to it for so many years of usefulness, as its teacher and guide. As it was a privilege to enjoy his ministrations, so the recollection of his faithful teachings and his faithful life should make us all stronger and more true to the work which God has assigned us.

At the age of ninety-three Dr. Nott was no longer able to perform the stated duties of the ministry, and Mr. George J. Harrison was ordained as Associate Pastor in March, 1849. Mr. Harrison is a native of Branford, and a graduate of Union College and Princeton Theological Seminary. His pastorate closed in October, 1851. In the month of May succeeding, (1852), Dr. Nott, at the age of ninety-eight, passed away to his reward.

The fifth pastor of the church was Rev. Jared R. Avery. He was educated at Williams College and Auburn Theological Seminary, and was installed as pastor in March, 1854. The following year was marked by a revival, as the fruits of which thirty-one were added to the church. Mr. Avery was dismissed in December, 1860.

The present pastor commenced preaching to this congregation in September, 1861, and was ordained February 4th, 1863.

This historic review should impress us with our *responsibility*, both for the religious privileges we enjoy, and for

---

* See Sprague's Annals of the American Pulpit, Vol. II, p. 190, &c.

the fulfillment of the duties we owe to the Redeemer's kingdom. From the generations past a precious inheritance has been handed down to us,—to pass on through our hand to generations yet to come. We should do something to enhance its value before we leave it to those who shall come after. Bonaparte kindled the martial ardor of his troops on the plains of Egypt by the cry, "From the summits of these pyramids forty centuries look down upon you." In a truer and nobler sense it may be said to us,—Four generations of those who here have toiled and prayed for the promotion of Christ's kingdom, look down upon you, to behold your fidelity to that sacred standard which they have upheld in many a conflict and now have bequeathed to you. May the remembrance of this cloud of witnesses stimulate us to fidelity in the work of God. May this commemorative day be not only one of joyous re-union and of hallowed memories, but one also of re-consecration to the service of Christ.

First Creed of the Church,

ADOPTED AT ITS ORGANIZATION, 1718.

— • ✦ • —

WE believe that there is one God, who is infinite, eternal and un-changeable in his being, wisdom, power, holiness, justice, goodness and truth; distinguished into three persons, the Father, the Son, and the Holy Ghost, the same in substance, equal in power and glory, and infinitely happy and blessed in the enjoyment of himself.

The Scriptures are the very and infallible word of God, containing all things necessary to salvation, being a perfect rule to direct and teach us what to believe and how to live.

God, from all eternity, hath decreed all things that come to pass in time.

In the beginning God made all things very good, and that in the space of six days, by the word of his power alone, and man in his own image and after his own likeness, with dominion of the creatures, whose body he made of the earth, into which he infused a rational soul or spirit, made immediately of nothing; and he does, by his most holy, wise and powerful providence, govern, guide and dispose of all creatures and things that he hath made, according to his sovereign and most absolute will and good pleasure.

Man, as he came out of the hands of God, was perfect and holy and happy; the estate wherein he was created was a sinless and blessed state. But he fell from it into an estate of sin and misery by sinning against God; for our first parents, being left to the freedom of their own will, hearkened to the temptation of the Devil and eat of the tree of knowledge of good and evil, contrary to the command of God; hence, sin entered into the world, and death, temporal, spiritual and eternal by sin; for Adam being constituted by God a public person, or one to act not only for himself but also for all his posterity, hence his sin and guilt became theirs.

Original sin, which consists in the want of original righteousness, and the corruption of the whole nature of man, constitutes, in part, the punishment of the first transgression, and hence arise all those actual transgressions which proceed from it.

God, of his mere good pleasure, elected some of the fallen children of men to everlasting life, and purposes to bring them out of the estate of sin and misery into an estate of grace and salvation by a Redeemer.

The Redeemer of God's elect is the Lord Jesus Christ, the eternal Son of God, according to the Scriptures, who in executing the Covenant of Redemption made between God the Father and himself, in due time became man by taking to himself a true body and a reasonable soul, and so was, and continued to be, two distinct natures in one person, forever.

Christ purchased salvation for the elect, or paid the price of their redemption unto God, by his active and passive obedience to the law in their stead and as their surety; and, as their Redeemer, sustains and executes the offices of a Prophet, of a Priest, and of a King. As a priest, he died for them, and therein offered the sacrifice of himself unto God for them, and makes intercession in heaven for them. As a prophet, he reveals the will of God and the way of life to them, in his Word and by his Spirit. As a King, he rose again from the dead, by his own power delivering himself out of the hands of death, and freeing himself from the power of the grave, and in a glorious and triumphant manner ascended up to heaven and set him down at the right hand of God the Father, and will judge the world at the last day, and subdues his people to himself, and restrains and conquers all his and their enemies.

Those that are elected are in due time effectually called. Effectual calling is the work of the Spirit which, by convincing us of our sin and misery, enlightening our minds in the knowledge of Christ and renewing our wills, doth persuade and enable us to embrace Jesus Christ freely offered unto us in the gospel. This embracing of Jesus Christ is saving faith, which faith is the great condition of salvation, and is ever accompanied with true repentance.

All that are effectually called are justified, adopted, and in this life sanctified, and glorified in the life to come. Those that are effectually called cannot either totally or finally fall from grace.

After death the bodies of men return to dust and see corruption, and their souls to God, who gave them. The souls of the righteous being then made perfect in holiness, do immediately pass into glory; their bodies being still united to Christ, do rest in their graves till the resurrection. And the souls of the wicked are cast into Hell, and there are reserved in chains of darkness till the judgment of the great day, when the souls and bodies of men will be re-united, and the righteous will be raised up in glory and shall be openly acquitted and made perfectly happy in the enjoyment of God forever; and then the wicked shall be filled with shame and contempt, and at the day of judgment shall meet the awful sentence of eternal damnation, and shall be banished from the face and presence of Christ forever into outer darkness, where they shall be tormented soul and body with fire and brimstone.

Concerning a particular church, we believe that it is a specific branch of a visible Catholic Church of Christ, consisting of several persons (who are the members thereof,) joining together to worship God in all the ways of his institution, or in all gospel ordinances. Church members have power of electing church officers, and when they have chosen them, ought to submit to them according to the rules of Christ, who is the King and head of the Catholic, and so of every particular church.

Concerning the Sacraments of the New Testament, we believe them to be two; viz., Baptism and the Lord's Supper, both of which are to be administered in every particular church of Christ by the ministers of the word; and they are holy ordinances instituted by Christ, wherein, by sensible signs, Christ and the benefits of his death are represented, sealed, and applied to believers.

Baptism is a sacrament wherein the washing with water in the name of the Father, Son, and Holy Ghost doth signify and seal our engrafting into Christ and partaking of the Covenant of Grace, and our engagement to be the Lord's. Baptism is to be administered to visible believers and their seed.

The Lord's Supper is a sacrament or holy ordinance instituted of Christ, wherein by giving and receiving bread and wine, according to the appointment of Christ, his death is showed forth, and they that worthily receive it, or partake as they ought, do therein by faith receive Christ himself, and in a spiritual manner feed upon his body and blood, broken and shed upon the cross for them, and so held forth, represented and offered thereby.

In testimony of our belief of the aforesaid Confession or Articles of faith, we subscribe:—

Henry Willes,	Thomas Hazzen,
David Hartshorne,	Samuel Edgerton,
Nathl. Rudd,	Samuel Ladd,
Joseph Kingsbury,	Joseph Kingsbury, Jun.

Note.—A second Confession of Faith, with a form of Covenant annexed, was adopted by the church soon after the commencement of Dr. Nott's ministry. It was, substantially, the same as the first, but much more concisely written, and was probably drawn by Dr. Nott himself. Much of the phraseology of this Confession having become obsolete, a *third* Confession of Faith and Covenant was adopted by the church, Nov. 5, 1865.

DEACONS OF THE CHURCH.

1718—Joseph Kingsbury,   *1741.

1718—David Hartshorne,   *1738.

1735—Feb. 20,—Joseph Kingsbury, Jun.,   *1757.

1735—Feb. 20,—John Durkee,

1759—Barnabas Huntington,   *1787.

1770—Ephraim Kingsbury,   *1772.

1777—Joseph Hunt,   *1786.

1786—Mar. 10,—Joshua Willes,   *1815.

1787—June 27,—Isaac Johnson.

1807—Jan. 2,—Phinehas Corwin.

1815—May 6,—Azariah Huntington,   *1833.

1816—May 3,—Samuel Allen,   *1826.

1824—Dec. 30,—Dyer McCall,   *1838.

1832—May 4,—Joseph Willes,   *1860.

1842—Mar. 4,—Nathaniel C. Greenslit, *1854.

1852—Mar. 5,—Benjamin S. Hastings,   *1859.

1853—July 3,—Ashbel Woodward.

1859—Sept. 2,—Henry N. Smith.

INTERMISSION.

At the close of the Historical Sermon, Rev. Elisha C. Jones, of Southington, led in prayer, after which the choir sang the hymn—

> "Lord God of Hosts, by all adored !
> Thy name we praise with one accord ;
> The earth and heavens are full of thee,
> Thy light, thy love, thy majesty."

The audience were then invited to adjourn to the adjacent town house, where the committee on collation, aided by the ladies of the society, had provided a

COLLATION

with bounteous abundance. Tables were arranged lengthwise of the building and loaded with ham, tongue, beef, sandwiches, biscuit spread with yellow Franklin butter, huge slices of Franklin cheese, and pies and cakes in great profusion. The ladies were determined to convince the returning wanderers that the old-time Franklin hospitality had suffered no decline, and that the tempting culinary arts of their mothers had been carefully preserved ; and no one questioned their success.

After the collation, about an hour was devoted to social converse, and many were the glad surprises which we noticed, as early friends unexpectedly met each other, and many the smiling faces as circles of former youthful intimates found themselves once more united. We saw one elderly gentleman running about with the eager hilarity of a boy, and searching for Capt. ———, whom he had not seen since they had played " H' I spy " together, around the wall of Deacon Willes' barnyard, fifty-three years ago the previous April.

The celebration probably produced a more general re-union of her absent children than Franklin had ever before witnessed. Not a few had come from distant states to be present at this occasion, and some were here who had never re-visited the town since their first departure from it, many years ago. The pleasure manifested by all these at being again among familiar sights and places, was a happy illustration of the force of local attachment and of the strength of the ties stretching from New England through the length and breadth of the land.

At three o'clock the bell again summoned to the church to the exercises of the afternoon.

———— • • • ————

The exercises of the afternoon were opened with the singing of the anthem, " Once more this day."

The pastor then read the following letter from the Hon. LaFayette S. Foster.

NORWICH, Oct. 12, 1868.

My Dear Sir :—I am exceedingly sorry not to be with you to-morrow. It is impossible for me not to be much interested in this celebration. Franklin is my birthplace ; those years of my life in which we form the strongest local attachments, were passed there, my maternal ancestors for several generations are buried there, many of my best and earnest recollections center there.

That I should be unable to be present and take some part in the exercises of the day is, I assure you, a matter of sincere regret. I trust and believe that your meeting may be both pleasant and profitable, and that in recurring to the past, the present generation may be stimulated to copy the examples of the wise and good who have gone before them, and so add luster to the history of the town which gave us birth. With kind and cordial greetings to the natives of our town, and to all who may join in the celebration,

My dear sir, very truly yours,

LaFAYETTE S. FOSTER.

Dr. A. Woodward.

The following letter from Bela Edgerton was then read :—

HICKSVILLE, OHIO, Sept. 17, 1868.

Ashbel Woodward, Esq.—Your note and the invitation to be present at the one hundred and fiftieth anniversary of the church and society of Franklin, has been duly received. I greatly regret that I cannot be present, as it would give me great pleasure to visit my native town once more. But my age and the infirmities incident to it forbid such a journey. That you may have a happy, good, and glorious time is my earnest prayer. Permit me to offer a sentiment :—

" FRANKLIN—The grave of my ancestors, the home of my childhood, the abode of a virtuous and honored people, long may their example be cherished, their puritan piety maintained unimpaired, and generations yet unborn follow the bright example.

I am, sir, respectfully yours,

B. EDGERTON.

N. B.—I am now eighty-two years old the present month.

B. E.

The following letter from the Rev. C. H. Chester was next read :—

GENEVA, N. Y., Sept. 7, 1868.

Mr. Ashbel Woodward, Chairman, &c.

Dear Sir.—I thank you for the invitation to be present at the one hundred and fiftieth anniversary of the Congregational church and society of Franklin. The name awakens pleasant memories. Though not myself a native of Franklin, but of Norwich, it was the birth-place of my sainted mother, and the home of my grand-parents.

Well do I remember, looking back more than forty years, the old " meeting house on the hill," plain even to plainness in its form and finish—no steeple, no bell the main entrance on the side fronting the green ; a door in each end ; large, square, and high-backed pews, made of chestnut wood, unpainted, and neither oiled nor varnished ; the pul pit high and narrow, with long winding stairs, trimmed with velvet ; the sounding-board on which I see now the quaint old figures, 1745 ; the galleries, (I recollect them well,) extending around three sides of the house, spacious and generally empty, a fine place for the tired farmer boys to stretch themselves out and have a good sleep ; the choir directly in front of the pulpit and over the main entrance, where, conspicuous, was that good man, Deacon Willes, with his tuning pipe ; and that venerable man of God, so slender, so spry, so queer in his dress—all these things are brought vividly to my recollection to-day. They have all passed away. They live only in our memories.

Allow me to note an incident connected with what, it seems to me, is the central figure in this celebration. It is a simple one, but it may serve to recall to some minds the long-lived and long-loved pastor of other days.

I was walking down the long hill leading from the meeting house, and had come to the foot of it, when, on looking before me, I saw the venerable Dr. in his buggy, approaching me. Between him and me were the school children who had just been let out for the night. As he came up to them he reined in his horse, and, removing his broad-brimmed hat from his head, he passed slowly through the ranks, waving it first to one side and then to the other, and so received the respectful and loving salutations of the young ones. It was a picture of patriarchal simplicity and grace which made an ineffaceable impression on my mind.

The old church has been, I am told, replaced by a new one. There is a new pastor, and, of course, since I, a boy, used to visit the place, a *new congregation*. "The fathers, where are they?"

May God bless both pastor and people, and make your anticipated gathering a holy convocation, fraught with pleasant memories, and full of promise for the years which are to come.

I regret that it will not be possible for me to be with you in person.

Yours, very respectfully,

C. H. CHESTER.

The poet of the day, Mr. Anson G. Chester, of Buffalo, N. Y., then delivered the following Poem.

POEM,

BY

ANSON G. CHESTER.

THE POEM.

It was in the dear old days,
    Days of earnest thought and labor,
Days when man, with soul and strength,
    Served his God and loved his neighbor—
When a simple faith and trust
    Lent to life a heavenly sweetness,
And its discipline of toil
    Gave it relish and completeness—
In those calm and quiet days,
    By a loving radiance gilded,
Here was set the ark of God,
    Here, in hope, a church was builded.

It was in the bloom and pride
    Of the old colonial season,
When the ruler's word and will
    Formed the sum of law and reason ;
When imperious Britain held
    All our treasures in her keeping,
And the beasts of after wars
    In their secret lairs were sleeping ;
When the godly Puritan
    Prayed, like Daniel, long and often,
And, responsive to his cries,
    Souls would melt and hearts would soften ;

When the hand was never closed,
  And the speech was frank and candid,
And the Sabbath Day was kept
  Holy, as its Lord commanded;
When the artless sermon sent
  Swift conviction to the hearer;
When, though life was dear and sweet,
  Yet was honor sweeter, dearer;
When the sturdy soul could pass
  Scatheless through the fires of passion—
When the very garb was cut
  In a modest, Christian fashion;
When the lips were free from guile
  And the breast from jealous burnings,
And the pious heart was thronged
  With immortal hopes and yearnings.

It was long before the hour
  When, in spite of regal minions,
Freedom bade her chosen bird
  Spread and try its eager pinions—
Penned the Charter of our Rights,
  With its bold, majestic phrases,
Wrote her matchless name in blood
  On the golden hearts of daisies!
When the grandest problem known
  Found its full and fit solution
Through the bayonet and the sword,
  In the glorious Revolution;
When a sweeter era dawned,
  And the days of king-craft ended,
And the gladsome songs of peace
  To the Lord of Peace ascended;

When began the proud career
  Of a calm, reliant nation,
Mighty through its trust in God,
  Up to Glory's loftiest station.

So they built the dear old church
  In the early days and pleasant,
Days that lend a roseate hue
  To the clouds that skirt the present:
Earnest, simple, pious men,
  Men who loved the Heavenly Master.
Men who feared the ways of sin
  More than danger or disaster—
Men to whom the Law was good
  And the Promise full of flavor,
Men who cared for riches less
  Than the Father's smile and favor.
Here, for years they heard the Truth,
  Here their tuneful praises proffered,
Here their willing alms they gave,
  Here, in faith, their prayers were offered;
Here their childrens' brows were wet
  With the sweet baptismal waters;
Here—for love is old as time—
  Here were wed their sons and daughters;
Here their honored clay was borne,
  When their earthly work was over,
And, the tearful service closed,
  Laid to rest beneath the clover.

Doubt not, while this church, to-day,
  O'er its wondrous past rejoices,
Doubt not that the dead are here
  With their angel harps and voices!

Though we see no golden stairs
   Reaching from the sapphire portal,
Though their shining forms are veiled
   From our vision, gross and mortal,
They have laid their crowns aside,
   They have come from heavenly places,
And their words are in our ears
   And their breath is on our faces!
They, the pioneers of God
   In a new and barren region—
Weak in numbers, but in faith
   Stronger than a Roman legion—
They who built and they who kept,
   They who planted, watched and tended,
They who since have lived and died
   In the faith their sires defended—
They, a glorious band, are here,
   Here to join our glad thanksgiving—
Rapturous must the worship be
   When the dead inspire the living!

Other dead than these have come
   From the shining hills above us—
Ah! it is a blessed thing
   That the saints may know and love us!
They who taught the earlier church
   Heavenly truths from holy pages—
Gave it manna from above,
   Water from the Rock of Ages;
They who ever loved to tell
   Calvary's sweet and blessed story—
First the thorns and then the gold,
   First the cloud and then the glory!
They whose words were words of peace,
   They whose lives were pure and holy,

They who warmed and clothed the poor,
 They who lifted up the lowly ;
Men of faith and men of prayer,
 Tender friends and zealous teachers—
Lo ! they take their rightful place
 Here among the living preachers.

One of these in life I knew,
 When my own was in its morning—
Oft I heard his Sabbath prayers,
 Oft his solemn Sabbath warning.
I can see the good man still,
 Clad in quaint and ancient vesture,
See his crown of silver hair,
 See his pleading look and gesture.
If his voice was heavenly soft
 While he spoke of Calvary's wonders,
When he laid the doctrines down
 It was clothed with Sinai's thunders !
If his heart was like a child's
 And his nature warm and pliant,
Question but his hope and faith
 And you roused a sleeping giant.
He could see the stamp of God
 On the meanest of His creatures,
In the homeliest Christian face
 Find celestial lines and features.
He was one who loved to strew
 Garlands on the paths of duty,
Loved in common things to seek
 For immortal truth and beauty ;
So he found—this good old man,
 Truest, saintliest, best of pastors—
Angels' eyes in violets,
 Bethlehem's tranquil star in asters ;

Found in leaf and brook and cloud,
    Found in nature's simplest forces,
Found in dew-drop, flake and fern
    Matter for his apt discourses.
Ah! the tears that he has wiped,
    Ah! the hearts that he has lightened,
Ah! the burdens he has shared,
    Ah! the lives that he has brightened.
Not a richer crown than his
    Flashes through the jasper arches
When the ransomed host of God
    Makes its grand and stately marches!
Brighter is its virgin gold
    Than the sheen of kingly sabres,
And its jewels are the souls
    Purchased by his pious labors.

What our fathers sowed in tears
    We, to-day, in joy are reaping—
Buried seed will sprout and grow
    While the husbandman is sleeping.
So this maniple of corn,
    Hid, in faith, upon the mountains,
Touched to life by power divine,
    Watered from celestial fountains,
Through the long and misty years
    Ever growing and increasing,
Shakes like Lebanon, at last,
    Lusty, ripe and full of blessing.

To the new and golden age
    Through a sterner age of iron,
Through the trial and the storm,
    God has led this reverend Zion :

Still His peace shall be her stay,
  Still His hand shall lead her surely—
Trusting to His love and care
  She shall ever walk securely.
List, O Zion, Bride of Christ!
  To the Psalmist's lofty numbers—
"He who keepeth Israel
  Never sleeps and never slumbers!"

Thou who rulest over all,
  Thou whose love all love excelleth,
Smile upon this holy place
  Where Thy sovereign honor dwelleth.

Thou our Refuge and our Rock,
  Thou our Maker, Friend and Father,
On this church, so full of years,
  Let Thy benedictions gather.

Give its pastor plenteous grace
  In his every work and function,
Guide his thoughts, inspire his words,
  Grant him holy zeal and unction;
May his labors bud and bloom
  Like the queenly rose of Sharon—
Give his deacons helpful hands,
  Like the hands of Hur and Aaron.

  May its members walk in love,
Doing all Thy will and pleasure—
  Fill their souls with heavenly peace
And their hearts with heavenly treasure.

  Take its infants in Thine arms
And its youth and children cherish—
  Let no lamb of all the flock
Stray from Thee, O God! and perish.

Give its men the fire of Paul,
　Abram's faith and John's emotion—
Give its women Esther's hope,
　Mary's trust and Ruth's devotion.

Of its aged be the staff
　Till to glory Thou hast borne them ;
Be the warden of its dead—
　Comfort Thou the hearts that mourn them.

Here may living waters flow,
　For the healing of the nation—
Make these hallowed portals praise,
　Make these sacred walls salvation.

And to God the King and Lord,
　Pitying Judge and Gracious Giver,
To the Father, Spirit, Son,
　Be the praise and power forever !

The delivery of the poem was followed by the singing of the anthem, " How beautiful in Zion," after which,

The Rev. Thomas L. Shipman, of Jewett City, spoke substantially as follows :—

There is one figure before us wherever we are to-day,—Dr. Nott. It makes me a better man only to think of him. I remember him well, for I have been acquainted with him many years. I recall many of his expressions in prayer. He was very pertinent and comprehensive in prayer. " May thy grace be sufficient for us and mighty in us." At " Minister's Meeting," he often had these petitions, but never too often, " May we love our Master and love our work." His style was char- acterized by great simplicity ; he came right to his subject, said what he had to say in simple Saxon, and when he had done, *stopped*. No man ever laid the sin of prolixness at the Dr.'s door. The Doctor was very much attached to the ministers' meeting. He was first to come, and first to leave at the close. The brethren would sometimes say to him, " Don't be in haste, Dr." His quick reply would be, "one duty follows another,—love to your families "; and before the brethren were ready to start he would be half a mile on his way home.

Towards the close of life, when his powers were much impaired, the family were unwilling that he should attend the meetings, fearing that some accident might befall him, and possibly that as he could not con- tribute to the interest of the meeting as he had done in former days, his presence might be an annoyance. If they ever entertained such an impression, I take this opportunity to disabuse them, for never was his presence more welcome. At the ordination of your present pastor, I shared the hospitalities of the family in the old parsonage. At the table I turned to my hostess and asked her if a story I had told and published of the Dr. was true. Her memory seemed very oblivious, but her husband, with a knowing wink whispered, " I guess it is true, for it sounds like them both." The story was to this effect.—At a certain time an invitation came up from Norwich to the Dr., to attend a Sabbath School celebra- tion of Independence. When the morning came, his grand-daughter took a seat in the carriage with him. The arrangement did not please the Dr. at all. " It's no place for women at ministers' meeting." " We are not going to ministers' meeting, we are going to celebrate the 4th of July." " It's no place for women, 4th of July, among the military." " There ain't going to be any military, it is a Sabbath School celebra- tion of Independence." He caught at the idea of independence. " I like independence, and women like independence too." " They don't

have much." " *They have quite as much as they can bear.*" If there
are any " Woman's Rights " brethren present, I crave their pardon, but
I was not willing to spoil a good story for their sakes.

Rev. Hiram P. Arms, of Norwich Town, followed, and
in a brief address, as pastor of the mother church, presented her kind salutations and hearty congratulations to
her first born daughter on the completion of her third
half century, to which were added some pleasant reminiscences of the late Dr. Nott.

Rev. Anson Gleason, formerly a missionary to the Choc-
taw Indians, and afterwards pastor of the Indian church
at Mohegan, gave some interesting reminiscences of his
first acquaintance with Franklin, and of his subsequent
ministerial intercourse with Dr. Nott.

Rev. David Metcalf next spoke and related quite a
number of anecdotes of early Franklin worthies, and
among them the following :—

When I was about to offer my services as a school teacher, I attended
in the fall of the year upon Mr. Nott's instruction about six weeks, with
a number of young men. The school room was Mr. Nott's study.
After recitation, one day, one of the young men rose and put on his
hat in Mr. Nott's presence. Mr. Nott said to him, " Young gentleman,
please take off your hat." He replied, " I thought school was done."
" I am the same man now that I was before," said Mr. Nott, and thus
that matter ended. At the close of the six weeks, I asked Mr. Nott if
he would give me a line of recommendation as a school teacher.
" Well," said he, " I can give you a line, but I shall not tell any lies
for you."

Rev. W. H. Moore next spoke briefly.

Rev. Jared R. Avery, of Groton, a former pastor of this
church, followed, and said—

Because of the lateness of the hour and the fact that others are to
address you, I shall speak with much brevity. For nine years, from
Nov. 1851, I ministered to this people. It constitutes *the* laborious
and happy period of my life. My services commenced six months
before the death of Dr. Nott. Much has been said of this venerable

man's punctuality and urbanity. Much may be said of his piety and his persistency for the right. He loved the sanctuary; and for the six months preceding his death, he failed of attending public worship only one and a half Sabbaths; it being the winter season of storms, and he 98 years old! Though unable to present formal sermons, he preached every day. At the close of the morning service on the last Sabbath he ever worshipped with the church militant, he addressed me in his peculiarly shrill voice, "Very well, sir, you have preached very well; but remember, we must beware lest, while we preach to others, we ourselves be castaways." To me that was a solemn sermon which I have often reviewed with trembling. Others have spoken of the toils and sufferings of pastors. I may speak of the joys and sorrows and kindnesses of the people. A revival of religion during my ministry has been alluded to in the historical discourse of the present pastor. It was a precious season, one of general interest, and as fruits of which, a goodly number were added to the church. There is a sadness mingled with our joys to-day, in review of the past. During my time of service, three deacons, Messrs. Greenslit, Willes and Hastings were removed by death; and many, many other loved ones of all ages. The two deacons of to-day were set apart to their office during the period of my ministry. This community's material tokens of kindness to their fifth pastor and his family continued to the last; and I can honestly say that I love to visit this people above any other, and take you by the hand, though that greeting be often attended by the falling tear.

Rev. Joseph W. Backus was next called upon. Mr. Backus, at the close of his remarks, produced some curious historical documents illustrating the rigorous manner in which the tything men fulfilled the duties of their office a century ago.

Rev. George J. Harrison, a former pastor of this church, and colleague of Dr. Nott, then spoke as follows:—

My acquaintance with this town commenced twenty years ago, about the middle of last month. The occasion of this acquaintance was as follows;—I received a letter from the respected chairman of your committee of arrangements, intimating that, in the opinion of the people, the venerable pastor of this church had fairly earned a period of rest, and that they were disposed to afford him relief from further labor by providing one who should be his assistant, and inviting me to come here in view of these facts.

One Sabbath morning I met and was introduced to Dr. Nott, at the large elm tree which stands at the corner, near Deacon Willes' house. He invited me to preach and I accepted the invitation. This was repeated several successive Sabbaths. At length the Dr. noticed my long continuance, and remarked to his grand-daughter " that he should think that Mr. Harrison had better be somewhere, seeking a place; that he could not afford to pay him anything, and he was sure that the people could not." His grand-daugher, in reply, informed him that the people proposed to provide him with a colleague. This statement the Dr. refused to believe.

Soon there was a call and acceptance; and in due season arrangements were made for an ordination. It was the pleasure of the people that this should occur on the 13th of March—the anniversary of the ordination of Dr. Nott. The day was a beautiful one, the air was soft, and great numbers came together from near and from far, attracted by the peculiar circumstances of the occasion.

Immediately after the completion of the usual services, the Dr. stepped forward and, in a few appropriate remarks, expressed his approbation of what had been done, and cordially thanked his people for their kindness in thus providing him with help. From that hour the entire charge of the parish was resigned into my hands, and it was with difficulty that Dr. Nott could be induced to perform the most trifling service. It was the desire of the people to hear his voice once on each Sabbath day. I therefore made it a point to invite him to offer the closing prayer of the afternoon; but only succeeded by the employment of a sort of strategy. As soon as I had finished the sermon, I would wave my hand to him as an invitation to offer the prayer, at the same time averting my eyes that he might not be able to decline.

The communion service, which would naturally have been observed on the first Sabbath of March, was deferred until the Sabbath after the ordination. Dr. Nott presided at the breaking of the bread; and those who were present will not easily forget the eminent propriety with which he concluded his portion of the service. Rising, and devoutly raising his hands towards Heaven, he commenced his address to the throne of grace with the following words : " O Lord, we are here in new circumstances. The senior pastor is present and the junior pastor is present." And so he proceeded, with that wonderful directness and appropriateness by which his prayers were always marked.

Mr. Thomas D. Stetson next spoke very briefly.

Rev. Jesse Fillmore followed, and spoke with much interest of his early recollections of Franklin.

Rev. Anson Gleason then led in prayer, after which was sung the hymn,—

> "Lord, now we part in Thy blest name,
> In which we here together came,
> Grant us, our few remaining days,
> To work Thy will and spread Thy praise."

The audience then joined in the doxology, and the exercises of the anniversary were closed with the

BENEDICTION.

Appendix.

A large number of interesting letters were received by the Committee of Arrangements from persons to whom invitations to the celebration had been extended. We append a few of these letters, regretting that the limits of the volume will not permit a more general collection.

We give first the letter of Miss F. M. Caulkins, of New London, who was invited to prepare a hymn to be sung at the opening of the anniversary exercises :—

NEW LONDON, Sept. 4, 1868.

Dear Sir :—

It gives me pleasure to hear of the proposed celebration at Franklin. I love these anniversary days. It does the heart good, sometimes, to turn aside and "ask for the old paths," especially *the path of the just* —that we may " *walk therein !'"*

My health is so fluctuating that I can scarcely hope for the gratifica- cation of personally presenting myself before this venerable *Hundred and Fiftieth.* But if health and other circumstances permit, I shall delight in being one of the train. In heart I shall certainly be there, nor shall the contribution so courteously requested be wanting. In the course of a few days I will forward a hymn.

Respectfully, sir, yours, &c.,

FRANCES M. CAULKINS.

Ashbel Woodward, M. D.

The Committee of Arrangements early invited Anson G. Chester, of Buffalo, New York, to deliver a poem at the celebration. Subjoined is Mr. Chester's letter of acceptance :—

BUFFALO, Sept 8th, 1868.

Dr. Ashbel Woodward, *Franklin Conn.*

Dear Sir:—I am in receipt of your letter, conveying to me the information that the Congregational church and society of Franklin propose
to celebrate the one hundred and fiftieth anniversary of their organization upon the fourteenth of October next, and inviting me to prepare
a poem to be read upon that occasion.

Franklin was the birthplace and early home of my beloved and
sainted mother; it was in the old church in Franklin that her infant
forehead received the sacred seal of baptism, and there in the years of
her maidenhood, she made profession of that faith which beautified all
her after life and rendered her death serene and triumphant; in Franklin she was married, and her children can testify that for Franklin, its
woods and fields, its church, its people, she cherished a love which never
languished, to the very moment when her mortal put on immortality.

So I seem to hear in your invitation the gentle pleadings of my
mother's voice—pleadings which, as of old and always, I hear but to
obey.

You may, therefore, expect me to be present at your celebration
and to bring with me such fruits, of the nature indicated in your very
kind letter, as in the meantime I may be able to gather.

With my grateful thanks to the committee for an invitation which is,
alike, complimentary in itself and its source, and which, while it whis-
pers pleasant things to my pride, touches the tenderest fibres of my
heart, I am,   Dear sir,

Very sincerely yours,

ANSON G. CHESTER.

SALEM, MASS., Oct. 13, 1868.

Ashbel Woodward, Esq., Chairman Com. of Arrangements, &c.

Dear Sir.—I received your very polite note inviting me to attend
your celebration of the one hundred and fiftieth anniversary of the
organization of your church and society, and I deeply regret it is not in
my power to be present.   Imperative official engagements which I cannot well control, prevent ; and I have delayed answering your note until
the last moment, in the hope that I could control them.   I certainly
feel a deep interest in the event to be commemorated, in which, and
in all your history to this day, my ancestors and kindred have taken no
inconsiderable part ; and I should be most happy to unite with you all
to-morrow in doing honor to the great and excellent many who have

rendered your annals as a church and a people, not undistinguished, and have given a name to Franklin of which you have no cause to be ashamed.

One name alone in your history, so loved and honored in the generations which he served, that of SAMUEL NOTT, deserves to be held in perpetual remembrance, and to be regarded as one of your most precious jewels on such an occasion as this, as well as at all times. He was widely and most honorably known in his long pastorate, and is largely identified with your history, and has given a prestige to the name and character of your town, as the minister of Franklin, not unlike to that given to your namesake town in this commonwealth by the long life and services in the ministry of Nathaniel Emmons, the minister of Franklin, Mass. All the names of the men and of the towns are great and good ; and your Franklin, a smaller one, was named, I presume, in honor of the great American statesman and philosopher. Again thanking you for your kind and considerate invitation to join in your celebration, which, I trust, and have no doubt, will be worthy of the event which you do well thus to mark, I remain,

Yours, very respectfully,

ASAHEL HUNTINGTON.

NORWICH, Sept. 17, 1868.

Doct. Ashbel Woodward, Chairman of the Committee.

Dear Sir:—I should take great pleasure in attending the celebration of the Congregational church and society in Franklin, in accordance with your invitation, but an engagement in another part of the state on that day will prevent.

It is a cause for great gratitude that for a century and a half the church has, in efforts to sustain a sound ministry, to secure the conversion of sinners to Christ, and to extend the interests of His kingdom in other lands, brought forth fruit to the glory and honor of the Master. That these efforts may continue and that the church may reflect, as it ever has, the light of the Gospel of the Son of God, is the prayer of your friend and obedient servant,

WM. A. BUCKINGHAM.

BUFFALO, October 5, 1868.

Dr. Ashbel Woodward, Chairman, &c.

Dear Sir :—I have delayed answering your note of invitation to attend the interesting celebration of your church on the 14th inst., in the hope that I might be able to send an acceptance of the same; but as I now see that it will not be practicable for me to be present, I will wait no longer, but express to you my thanks for the invitation and my sincere regret that I cannot be present to share in the festivities and solemnities of that occasion.

Though not a son of Franklin, I am a grandson, and many precious early memories cluster about that locality. In the old church, not the oldest, my father, a native of the neighboring town of Montville, saw by chance in the choir, my mother, the eldest child of Major Eleazar Tracy, the eldest, by the way, of fourteen girls and boys,—they had families in those days,—my father's father was the eldest of sixteen children,—and the black hair and bright eyes of the youthful Prudie were too much for him; he yielded at once, and the next year, in 1811, Dr. Nott was sent for to heal the wound that love had made. This event had quite an important bearing upon my history, and gives to the Franklin meeting house a personal interest that I can never lose. Very often, in my childhood and early youth, in my visits to my grandfather, have I attended service in the old church, and most vividly do I recall the appearance and voice of the pastor who for so many years ministered to this flock. I had then the veneration for the minister, which has to so great an extent disappeared in this age, and which will be of no loss, if we do not also lose veneration for the religion which the minister represented.

I am sorry I cannot come, but I send my youngest brother, who shall speak for us both in his graceful verse, inspired by the love of the dear, departed mother, with whose blessed memory Franklin, and especially the Congregational church in Franklin, will ever be associated.

Very gratefully and truly yours,

A. T. CHESTER.

————

AURORA, ILLINOIS, Oct. 7th, 1868.

To Ashbel Woodward, Chairman Com. of Arrangements.

Dear Sir:—Your circular, inviting me to be present at the celebration of the one hundred and fiftieth anniversary of the organization of the church and society in Franklin, was received in due time.

I thank you for the invitation. I sympathize with the sentiment which prompts to such a celebration. It is well to bind the present to the past with ties of grateful remembrance. The full stream may not despise the little spring whence it took its rise. The generation of to-day ought not to think lightly of the work of their fathers, which is the very spring of their present prosperity, that patient industry which has changed the sterile hills of old Franklin into fruitful fields ; that frugality which has gathered plenty from a reluctant soil ; that sobriety and virtue which have adorned, and still adorn, so many happy homes ; that substantial piety which has given strength and dignity and grace to so many unheralded lives, and has crowned them with peace at their ending ; all have been due beyond measure to the presence of that little church on Meeting House hill. I am glad you are to recall the past and set in honor those who in by-gone years wrought for the results which are the rich inheritance of those living to-day.

It is well, too, by such a review to learn more fully the lesson of God's faithfulness and love. Above man's agency is God's blessing. That blessing has been the best thing in the past history of the church ; that constitutes the chief worth of the inheritance which the present possesses. To make grateful acknowledgement of God's goodness, and to secure larger measures of his blessing, will doubtless be one chief object of your anniversary exercises. I regret that it is quite impossible for me to be with you. Distance and pressure of duties will prevent my coming. Thanking you again for your invitation, and wishing you all hoped for success in the proposed celebration, I remain,

Yours, very sincerely,

ISAAC CLARK.

POEM,

FROM MISS HYDE,

OF

Andover, Conn.

October, 1718.
October, 1868.

Their graves are with us to this day,
  With hillock green and mossy stone,
Whose crumbling records pass away,
Whose memory we would guard for aye,
  Heirs of the work they here begun.

So to this hilltop's ancient shrine
  Our pilgrim feet to-day repair;
Grateful we trace the ancestral line,
And own the covenant divine,
  Whose blessings we so richly share.

This day, for their memorial claimed,
  To kindred ties and greetings given,
Tells of the rest which they have gained,
Gathered to Him, of whom are named
  The family of earth and heaven.

Index of Names.

A

ABELL, Abigail, 72; Alpheus, 38; Benjamin, 49; Caleb, 49; Experience, 56; Joshua, 17, 21, 26, 40, 42, 62; Julietta, 73; Mary, 63; Simon, 38.

ADGATE, Hannah, 52; Dea. Thomas, 48.

AITCHISON, Rev. William, 88.

ALLEN, Dea. Samuel, 112.

ALLYN, Edward A., 62; Elizabeth, 63; Secretary John, 46; Robert, 48.

ANDREWS, Christian, 51.

ARMS, Rev. Hiram P., D.D., 10, 130; Rev. Wm. F., 88.

ARMSTRONG, Asa, 38; Benjamin, 17, 21, 25, 49; Benjamin, 2d, 38; Jeremiah, 38; John, 17, 21, 25, 49; Jonathan, 49; Joseph, 49; Stephen, 49.

ARMSTRONGS, 32.

ARNOLD, John, 49.

ARNOLD PLACE, 22, 50.

ASHBURY, Rev. Bishop Francis, 70.

ATTAWANHOOD, son of Uncas, 45, 46.

AVERY, Christopher, 36; Rev. David, 64, 65, 66, 68; Rev Ephraim K., 87; John, 65; Lydia (Smith), 65; Rev. Jared R., 107, 130.

AYER, Bailey, 92; E. Eugene, 5; John, 15, 50, 85; Joseph, 21, 25, 38; Joseph, Jr., 25, 38, 50, 66; Love, 57, 85; Mary (Bailey), 66; Rev. Oliver, 65, 66; Timothy, 38.

AYERSES, 32.

AYER'S GAP, 50.

10

B

H

K

KINGSBURY, Andrew, 57 ; Capt. Asa, 85 ; Ephraim, 57, 80, 112 ; Eunice,
51 ; Col. Jacob, 39, 57, 85, 86 ; Hon. John, 57, 64 ; Jonathan,
64 ; Dea. Joseph, Sen., 25, 57, 85, 111, 112 ; Dea. Joseph, Jr.,
25, 33, 57, 111, 112 ; Dr. Obadiah, 80 ; Sanford, 64.
KINGSBURYS, 32.
KINGSLEY, Charles A., 5, 6 ; Henry W., 5, 6, 49 ; Jason W., 63, 79 ;
John, 38 ; Samuel, 38 ; Col. Thomas G., 51.
KNOWLTON, Col. Thomas, 39, 83.

L

LADD, Abner, 38 ; Rev. Beaufort, 65, 74 ; David, 21, 25, 38, 57 ;
David, 38, 58 ; David, 38 ; Erastus P., 55 ; Ezekiel, 38, 57 ;
Henry L. M., 55 ; Jonathan, 25 ; Joseph, 57 ; Joseph D., 57 ;
Nathaniel, 25, 57 ; Samuel, 25, 111 ; Samuel, Jr., 38.
LADDS, 32.
LAMB, Guilbert, 53.
LANGLY, Sims, 25.
LATHROP, Barnabas, 38 ; Elijah, 82 ; Israel, Sen., 58 ; Sergt. Israel, Jr ,
22, 25, 58 ; Jesse, 58 ; Capt. John, 22, 58 ; Rev. John, of Lon-
don and afterwards of Scituate and Barnstable, 58 ; Rev. John,
D.D., of Boston, 58 ; Leander, 38 ; Samuel, 58 ; William, 58.
LATHROPS, 32.
LEDYARD, John, 36.
LEE, Jane, 56 ; Rev. Joseph, 90 ; Thomas, 56.
LEFFINGWELL, Elizabeth, 63 ; Lieut. Thomas, 48.
LORD, Alethea, 71 ; David N., 64 ; Dr. Elisha, 71 ; Rev. Nathan L.,
M.D., 88.

M

MANWARING, Rev. William H., 88.
MARSHALL, O. H., 65.
MASON, Dorothy (Hobert), 58 ; Edward, 62 ; James F., 58 ; Jeremiah,
22, 58 ; Col. Jeremiah, 87 ; Hon. Jeremiah, 35, 58, 64, 87 ;
Major John, 14, 15, 46, 48, 58, 87.
MASONS, 32.
M'CALL, Dea. Dyer, 41, 112 ; Lucy, 41.

T

U

W

Y